Sarey by Lantern Light

Sarey by
Lantern Light

Written & Illustrated by
Susan Williams Beckhorn

 DOWN EAST BOOKS / Camden, Maine

ISBN 0-89272-612-1
LCCN: 2003107746
Design: Northeast Corner Design
Printed at P. A. Hutchison Co., Mayfield, Penn.

2   4   5   3   1

Down East Books
Book orders: 1-800-685-7962
www.downeastbooks.com

To my wise and kind brother, David,
and to every kid who has ever struggled

❦ One ❦

"SARAH HARRIS, THAT'S DISGUSTING!"

Twenty-nine pairs of eyes turned to look. Sarey's face burned with embarrassment. She had only been crossing her eyes. That wasn't disgusting. Mikey Greenbaum showing his double-jointed thumbs was disgusting. Well, she was bored. Ma and Pa had read her all the A. A. Milne books long ago. She would always love them, but didn't her teacher know that *Winnie-the-Pooh* was way too baby a book for her class?

"Do you think you could do a *better* job of reading, Sarah?" Mrs. Carver led Sarey to the front of the room and put the book into her hands. "Two paragraphs, if you please, starting here," her teacher said in a cold voice.

Something like dead fish soaked in sour milk rose up in Sarey's stomach. Mrs. Carver knew exactly how hard it was for her to read. Sarey clutched the book to keep herself from falling. The words were jiggling, wavering, flickering. She felt all those eyes on her, could actually feel the sensation on her skin of everyone looking, could actually feel the sensation on her skin of everyone looking. She tried to see the words, to say them, to make them stand still. A hoarse, shaky sound was all that would come out of her mouth. Inside, her voice was painfully clear, screaming, *I CAN'T! PLEASE DON'T MAKE ME!* But she couldn't scream it out loud, even to save herself.

Suddenly, Sarey dropped the book and found she was running. She didn't stop when Mrs. Carver called down the corridor after her. She didn't stop for her coat, or anything. Sarey ran out of school and across intersections with cars honking at her all the ten blocks home to the apartment on Mill Street. She would *never*, even if she lived to be a hundred and thirty-seven, read again.

After the principal called her at work, Ma found Sarey. She was in the yard hugging their big dog, Oakley, still sobbing.

"I won't read, Ma."

"Sarey, you can do it." Ma found a packet of tissues in her purse, pulled out three or four, and handed them to her.

Sarey blew her nose. It was hard to get the words out. "I'm in . . . the lowest reading group still . . . and I hate extra reading class with Mr. Plaisted . . . and Ma, Mrs. Carver dragged me up in front

of the whole class and tried to make me read out loud today. I can do it slow with Mr. Plaisted, but not in front of everybody! They'll think I'm stupid. I get sick feeling . . . like I'm going to fall down. I can't see the words straight."

Ma pulled Sarey's head onto her shoulder and didn't say anything. Oakley leaned against Sarey and licked her wet face anxiously.

"I'm just dumb."

"No, Sarey, you are not dumb."

"I'm not ever going to read again," she said, and she meant it.

For as long as she could remember, Sarey and her parents had wanted to move away from Buffalo. Once in a while, Ma made a picnic lunch, Pa let Oakley off his chain, and they drove out to the country, away from the city and the bad-smelling air that poured from the factories beside the big lake. In the city, the bare ground between the cracked pavement was hard. In the woods and fields, Sarey could take her shoes off and feel the ground springy and alive under her feet. Even the sky was wide and alive instead of closed and gray.

"I'm a country boy," Pa would tell her, "but when Gramma and Grampa lost the farm, we came to Buffalo. Been here ever since. I get lonely for the woods, hungry for them, like Oak on his chain. Someday . . . " Pa sat up and his eyes sparkled like sun on water. "Someday, we'll get some money saved, Sarey. I'll find a teaching job in the country and we'll build a house."

"And I'll have my own room."

"You'll have your own room."

Sarey closed her eyes and let the dream make a bright picture in her mind. She saw her own room with sunlight streaming in at the window and pink curtains stirring in the breeze. There would be lots of shelves for her things. She would put her best drawings on the walls, ones of horses maybe. . . .

"And we can have a garden," Ma had added wistfully, "and walk in the woods whenever we want." Ma was a country person, too. She had grown up outside of Boston, but had spent childhood summers in New Hampshire.

"And you can go to a school that's not overcrowded, one where everybody knows your name. And Oakley can live like a dog ought to live. . . . "

Oakley was part collie and part malamute. His fur was long and golden with black tips. The house Sarey and her parents were living in was cut up into four apartments and looked like all the others on their street, and on all the other streets in their part of the city, but there was a scrap of yard with a maple tree. They could keep a dog. That was *something*. At night Oakley came inside, but during the day he paced a hard, bare circle on the end of his chain around his doghouse in the yard. The collie in him loved people, but his malamute blood ran hot and wild. In Buffalo, he never carried his tail up over his back or pranced the way he did when he was in the woods.

The night after Sarey ran away from school, she overheard Ma and Pa talking in the kitchen. She was not eavesdropping. It was just that she could hear when they talked in the kitchen because her room was really the living room. They thought she was asleep.

"What kind of English teacher can't teach his own daughter to read?" Pa's voice sounded twisted up tight, like a wet towel. "I wish I understood dyslexia better. They didn't really teach us much about it in school. I guess they figured that high school English teachers don't have to deal with it, that it mostly gets ironed out by the reading teachers in the primary grades. I just wish those so-called reading experts could come up with some better solutions. There must be a key to this."

Ma's voice was calm. "You know there is no magic treatment,

Dan, but there are strategies she can use, and there are ways of compensating. Sarey has to accept that and be willing to do the work. Her listening skills are good. We should be grateful for that. Some kids don't even process spoken words well. Right now, it's like she's growing underground. We don't see anything on the surface, but we've got to believe that, inside, she's listening and learning."

"Well, plants need space—earth, sunlight, air! Some kids do fine in a big city school, but Sarey's not like that. She needs a place where she doesn't have to talk loudly to be heard, a place where she can be herself but still be a part of things. This is it, Ellen. None of us are happy here. We're getting out of Buffalo."

Sarey's eyes opened wide in the dark. Getting out of Buffalo! She pulled the covers up around her neck carefully so her feet wouldn't poke out at the bottom. Her bed was really the living room couch during the day. Ma had to make it up for her every night, which wasn't so easy, even when they sort of rolled the sheets and blankets up together in a bundle to save time. It never was as smooth and comfortable as a real bed. Something was always bunching up or sliding off. Sarey's clothes were in a dresser in the hall. She didn't even have a shelf for her toys and special stuff. They had to be kept in a box in the closet. What she wanted, almost as much as she didn't want to ever read again, was her very own, nobody-can-walk-in-anytime room.

"I could quit the job at the library and get something full time," Sarey heard Ma say. "Then, maybe in a year or two we would be in a better position—"

"Ellie, I don't want you to do that," Pa interrupted her. "I think there's more to Sarey's reading problems than just seeing letters backward and mixing up right and left. She's a really special kid, but not in a bad way—in a good way. I just think she's in the wrong environment. Or maybe her problems come from being stuck with a set of parents who hate where they live."

Sarey reached down and scratched Oakley's ears. Usually he would sleep here on the rug beside her while Ma and Pa did their evening work at the kitchen table. Pa would be correcting papers, and Ma would be proofreading something. She was always writing something when the housework was done. Sometimes she read her stories to Sarey at bedtime. They were for younger kids, really, but Sarey thought they were pretty good. She especially liked the one about the bear cubs, Tubbs and Chubley, who tried to mail a fish home from summer camp in July. Ma's cheeks would get pink when she read one of her own stories, and she would glance up at Sarey every few lines, almost as if she was afraid Sarey might think her story was boring. It seemed funny to be just a kid trying to encourage her own ma, but none of the magazines Ma sent her stories to seemed to want them, so somebody had to tell her that they were still good stories.

Sarey gave Oakley's head another pat. She knew that if she woke up later in the night, she'd find the kitchen light off and Oakley gone. He would have followed Pa into the bedroom to sleep at the foot of the bed. He loved them all, but he was really Pa's dog.

The thought of waking up in the dark alone brought that old achy, lonely feeling, and for the millionth time, Sarey wished she had a little sister. She was sure she would like a sister, but when she asked, Ma would look away and say, "We don't always get babies when we want them, Sarey." Then Ma would hug her and say, "Pa and I are so lucky to have you, kiddo."

Sarey flipped her pillow over so the cool, fluffy part was under her neck. Getting out of Buffalo! Did Pa really mean it? She thought about never having to walk in the front door of Elm Street School again. Never having to raise her eyes to meet Mrs. Carver's again. It would be like dancing in the rain after a summer-long drought. She could almost feel the dried, caked dust of bad feelings washing away. Surely a new school, a little school in the country, would be better.

The voices in the kitchen continued. She heard Ma say, "Dan, rural schools have their own problems. Who's to say she'll get the help she needs there? In another year or two we will have saved what we planned. Maybe we should wait."

"No," Pa answered. His voice was quiet and firm. "It's time for us to go."

Sarey slipped off the couch, put her arms around the big dog's neck, and buried her face in his glossy fur. "Oakley," she whispered, and her voice quivered with the unbelievableness of it. "We're getting out of Buffalo!"

❧ Two ❧

BUT IT WASN'T AS EASY AS ALL THAT. The next day, Sarey came home
with a note from Mrs. Carver because she would not read the questions on her history test, and if you wouldn't read the questions,
how could you, even in your crawling, scrawling, misspelled hand-
writing, answer them?

"Sarey, I think you know this material," said Pa sternly, looking over the copy of the test that the teacher had enclosed.

"I'm not going to read. I told you that," Sarey said hotly.
"Anyway, it doesn't matter, because we're getting out of Buffalo!"

Her parents glanced quickly at each other, and Ma said, "Oh,
but Sarey, there's the rest of the year still to go. Your father can't
just up and leave his job in April. You'll never get through school
anywhere if you don't read."

"You said there's lots of people in the world who can't read,
but they get along somehow. You said they develop their memo-
ries so they don't have to read. I'm just going to be illiterate, and
get along."

"Well, that's a possibility, Shorty," said Pa, his eyes twinkling.
"You *are* pretty smart, even if you're no bigger than a question

mark. Humans can keep amazing amounts of information inside their heads. I've heard that some tribal elders have hundreds of years of their people's history memorized."

Ma rolled her eyes at Pa. "Anyone who is smart enough to call herself 'illiterate' is smart enough to learn to read!"

They tried to trick her. "Is that Washington Street up ahead?" Ma asked one afternoon as she drove Sarey to the dentist.

Sarey would not look up.

"Here's a card from Uncle Rich. He always has something funny to say—but I left my specs in the truck. Can you read it to me, Shorty?"

Sarey stalked out to the truck and fetched Pa's glasses.

"Does the recipe say to stir or fold in the dry ingredients?" Ma asked her when they were baking a cake.

But just looking at words made Sarey's stomach tighten. She would not be tricked.

There were long, dreadful hours sitting on a chair in the principal's office—but she still would not read. There was a conference with teachers, which Sarey was not invited to, and a conference with the school psychologist, which Sarey *was* invited to. The psychologist finally looked over her glasses at Ma and Pa and said, "I'm afraid this is going to take a little time. A fresh start may help, but in the end, this is up to Sarey."

Except for art, music, and gym, Sarey's grades nose-dived. Ma said, "Sarey, you were learning. It's hard for you, but you were making progress. Sometimes a teacher doesn't understand when one of the fish in her school swims fast in some ways and slow in others. She expects you all to be the same. You can't just stop trying." But Sarey could, indeed, stop trying.

Ma and Pa tried not reading to Sarey anymore, but after two miserable weeks, they gave in and once again read to her at bedtime, just as they always had. Sarey had never stopped wanting to *listen* to stories. Listening was so easy for her. "It's better than nothing," Sarey heard Pa mutter to Ma. It was cozy, and she could see it all just as if Big Red or Black Beauty were outside under the streetlight, peeking in the window and looking over their shoulders. When they tried to get her to do it herself, she turned wooden. Even if she had been willing to try, Sarey knew what would happen. The black lines that were supposed to make letters and words would run backward and inside out and get all tangled up. They would not mean anything. It would make her feel sick and like she was falling.

At Easter break, Ma and Pa took Sarey over to stay at Gramma and Grampa's house.

"How's my favorite grandchild?"

Sarey giggled inside Grampa's bear hug. "Grampa, I'm your *only* grandchild."

"Still one in a million."

"We're sorry to miss the holiday," said Pa to Gramma.

Gramma smiled brightly as she looked at Sarey. "It will be special with just the three of us. We know how important this trip is to you."

Pa and Ma went by themselves way up to Aroostook County in northern Maine, almost into Canada. When they got back, they were excited. "It's so big, they just call it 'the County,'" Pa told Sarey. There's a job for an English teacher opening up next fall at a little school near Caribou—and they said I could have it. *And* we bought thirty acres of land from a potato farmer named Ed Willette. Mr. Willette said we could stay in his hunting cabin in the woods near the property he sold us. We can live in it rent-free while we build our house, because he doesn't use it all that much. It's potato country," said Pa, giving Sarey a squeeze. "Lots of room to grow!"

Sarey looked from one happy, smiling parent to the other. Now maybe everything would be good.

"We'll build a house and live in the woods. We'll get back to the land and be self-sufficient, and things will be better for you," Pa said. "You'll still have to go to school, but it will be better. I know it will."

Then came the planning and packing. There were things to give away, things to sell. "We can't afford to rent a van," Ma explained to Sarey, "so we can only take whatever will fit in the truck." One Saturday, Sarey and Ma helped Pa build a camper out of plywood and roofing paper over the bed of their old truck. In the back it had a door with a window in it.

"It looks like a little barn," Sarey said.

"We'll be sort of like homesteaders going out West in a covered wagon," said Pa. "Only we'll be going in the other direction."

They packed the camper full of boxes of clothes, blankets, books, Pa's tools, and Ma's typewriter and guitar. Sarey loved the jumbled way the truck looked when it was all packed.

The school year was finally over, and Sarey had brought her report card home without even looking at it. She knew she had failed. The word made her stomach queasy, but not as sick as reading made it feel.

"You'll have to repeat a grade," said Ma with a sigh, "but the kids at your new school won't know you were held back. Everything will be easier."

Sarey's jaw tightened. She still was not going to read. Not ever.

It was time to go. It was hard to say goodbye to Gramma and Grampa Harris. "But we'll come visit when we can, and write," Gramma said. "And you'd better write back!"

Sarey nodded and swallowed. How could she tell Gramma that she wasn't going to read her letters, much less try to answer them?

"I thought maybe you could use this," said Grampa. He handed Pa the kerosene lantern that he called Old Joe. It was one of the last things left from the farm.

"Thanks," said Pa. His voice sounded like it was hard to talk. He hung Old Joe on a nail just inside the door of the camper.

Finally, they got in the truck and drove away from Buffalo and out onto the New York Thruway. The road seemed to go on forever. Sarey watched the steady streams of cars traveling east and west and thought about all her years of school so far.

Back in kindergarten, she had been more interested in drawing pictures than learning her letters and numbers. She drew Mr. and Mrs. Dinosaur taking their little one to school, the mermaid's underwater tea party, and the Scalawag family history. Sarey was the smallest in her class, and she didn't say much. The other kids liked her drawings, but after a while they got tired of trying to get her to talk. Then Marla Simmons, who was taller even than some of the second graders, started calling her Baby, and pretty soon the other girls, who followed Marla around like she was a mother duck, did it, too.

First grade, when she was supposed to have learned to read, had been okay. That was because of Mrs. Mallory. Sarey could remember sitting at a little round table with Mrs. Mallory, Ma, and Pa, talking about reading. It had not seemed like such a big thing then. She remembered exactly what Mrs. Mallory had said: "I think maybe Sarey's head is already so full of stories of her own, and she can express them so beautifully in her drawings, that she's just not interested in reading and writing yet. I'm sure it will come in good time." Then she had added, "You know, Mr. and Mrs. Harris, I have never seen a child draw like Sarey, not in twenty-three years of teaching. I ask her where she gets her ideas, and she answers, 'I get them from my dreams.' She truly has a gift—but sometimes gifts come with a little challenge, too."

Now Sarey shifted restlessly on the seat of the truck between her parents, closed her eyes, and tried to fall asleep, but without wanting to, she remembered her next teacher, Miss Cullen. "Stop drawing and pay attention!" she said over and over again to Sarey in her sour-lemon voice. One time, she rapped her chalk on Sarey's desk until it snapped and then huffed angrily back to her desk for a new piece as if it had been Sarey's fault. Miss Cullen scolded her for handing in papers with decorated margins and picture stories on the back. She made the class do endless color codes, where every shape with numbers in it that added up to seven had to be colored blue, and each shape where the numbers added up to eight had to be colored orange, and so on. They had to stay in the lines, and it took up a lot of time. Why couldn't they just add up the numbers and be done with it? What Sarey really wanted to do was to draw her story about the little dragon, Fire, and his baby sister, Pokey (who was called that because she couldn't say her own name, Smoke, yet). She didn't need to practice staying within the lines. She could already do that.

By the end of second grade, Sarey could barely stumble through the easiest books, and the other kids got really quiet or even snickered whenever she was called on to read. This past year, with Mrs. Carver, Sarey's stomach would knot up, the letters would jiggle, and she couldn't read at all.

Once, Sarey said to Ma, "I'm not like the other kids."

Ma pushed Sarey's hair back from her forehead gently and said, "None of us is just like everyone else, Sarey, except that each of us has troubles of our own."

"I'm the only one who doesn't have a best friend, and nobody ever picks me for a partner."

"Maybe you should do some of the picking instead of waiting to be chosen."

Sarey was too busy feeling sorry for herself to listen. "I'm still the smallest, and they still call me Baby," she said, sniffing.

"Sarey, someone's got to be the smallest, and you remember the old saying about sticks and stones. You're plenty big enough. Pay no attention to them."

Sarey twisted around to look through the back window into the camper to see how Oakley was doing. He was sound asleep with his chin propped on a box of kitchen utensils. It didn't look too comfortable, but Oakley didn't seem to mind.

Ma was studying a map. "What time will we get to Boston?" Sarey asked. Ma's parents lived near that city, and they were planning to stop there overnight along the way.

"We should be able to make it by dinner time," Pa answered.

Dinner time? They hadn't even had lunch yet! Sarey wriggled in her seat.

"Best thing for boredom on a trip is a good book," said Ma.

Sarey stiffened. "I'm not bored," she said crossly.

Ma's parents laughed when they saw the truck. "It looks like a gypsy wagon," said Grandmother Potter. That sounded nice—

Sarey thought of a wagon all painted with flowers and birds, pulled by a prancing pony—but it seemed like Ma's parents did not really like the truck, because Grandfather Potter asked Pa to park around the corner where the neighbors wouldn't see it.

They didn't seem enthusiastic over the move to Maine, either. "It's pretty isolated up there," said Grandfather as he served them roast beef in the fancy dining room.

"And just as far away as Buffalo," added Grandmother, her perfectly curled silver hair gleaming in the candlelight. "We wish you would stay a while and not leave tomorrow."

Sarey saw Pa steal a glance at Ma. "You know we would love to, Mom, but we'll be building a house," said Ma. "We've already had to wait until the end of the school year, and summer is shorter up there, with school starting in August so the kids can help with the potato harvest in the fall."

"Am I going to pick potatoes, Ma?" asked Sarey.

"Ellen, I wish you wouldn't let Sarey call you and Dan Ma and Pa," said Grandmother Potter. "This is not the eighteen hundreds!" Pa's eyes twinkled at Sarey, but he said nothing. Sarey saw that Ma's cheeks had suddenly grown pink, and she was staring at her plate.

Grandmother made a clucking noise with her tongue, and Sarey sensed her disapproval. "I just don't understand this hippie notion of moving out to the middle of nowhere and building your own house. What's wrong with living like normal people in a normal house?"

Ma set down her fork and looked up. "We think people have grown too separate from the land—too dependent on the system. Nobody does things for themselves anymore. Kids don't even know where the food they eat comes from or how it's grown. There is something wonderful about making things with your own hands, whether it's a loaf of bread, a shirt, or even a house.

Oh, I know there will always be some things we need to buy, but Dan has a good job waiting. It's just something we want to do, Mom. It'll be an adventure."

Sarey saw her parents exchange another uncomfortable glance.

Coming up along the coast of Maine, they camped out one night and ate clams steamed over the campfire while they listened to the ocean sounds. Ma played her guitar, Pa played his harmonica, and they sang a song that Ma had written:

When the hills go dark, and the home lights are gleaming,
And the good dogs bark, and he's standing in the door,
Then I'll kiss the kids in their beds where they lie dreaming.
There's a blessing in a winter storm and getting home once more.

Ma worried that the exhaust from the truck would make Oakley sick riding in the camper, but the new plank floor that Pa had built over the rusted bed of the truck was solid and tight. They drove for miles and miles and hours and hours. Maine was so much bigger than Sarey had ever imagined! Finally, in the afternoon of the third day since leaving Buffalo, Pa pulled off the highway and followed a twisty little gravel road for several miles. They rattled over a small bridge. Just beyond that, there was a turning-off place.

"We're here!" Pa exclaimed, as he parked the truck. They all piled out and opened the door in the camper to let Oakley out, too. He scrambled to the ground, wagging all over, eager to see where they were now.

❧ Three ❧

"WHY IS THERE A ROAD GOING INTO THE WOODS?" asked Sarey.

"It was probably made by loggers when they cut timber here years ago," Pa answered. "There are old logging roads all over the north woods. If this one were not so grown over and rough, we could drive up it."

"No sense going empty-handed!" Ma said, picking up a box of groceries. Pa slung Old Joe over his arm and took one of the boxes of kitchen stuff because that was the heaviest. Sarey carried an armful of blankets. Oakley just pranced and woofed with his tail wagging up over his back.

"Too bad you can't at least carry your own dog food," Ma told him, but she smiled, watching him play. The trail led them up through bigger woods. In some places there were deep, old ruts filled with rainwater, and they had to walk in the middle and on the edges to keep their feet dry. In other places, young balsam firs had grown in thickly so that they almost had to push their way through. They stepped over logs and fallen branches. Sarey's arms began to ache, but she didn't want to set the blankets down and get leaves and pine needles on them. "Are we almost there?" she panted.

"Just a little farther, Shorty," said Pa.

Finally, when Sarey thought her arms might let go of the blankets all by themselves, they came to a cabin next to a tumbling brook. It was just a small, rectangular building of weathered boards, with windows that didn't match, but there was something about it that made Sarey grin when she saw it. "It's the Little House in the Big Woods!" she said. Then, "I have to go to the bathroom."

"Follow me!" said Pa. He set his box on the front steps and put the blankets on top of it. Then he headed around the side of the cabin to a rickety-looking structure out back under the trees. He opened the door, and Sarey saw an old wooden toilet seat set into a sort of bench. There was a roll of toilet tissue under a tin can.

"I'm supposed to go in there?" she asked.

"That's it, Shorty!" said Pa. "You've seen an outhouse before."

Soon after, when they pushed open the creaky door of the cabin and stepped inside, there was a scurrying of many tiny feet.

"Looks like the squirrels and mice have taken over," said Pa with a chuckle. It was dim inside. Pa lit the lantern so they could see better. Close to the door was a kitchen area with a sink, counter, and cupboard. There was a comfortable sitting area with a wood stove and table and chairs. A double bed stood in the far corner. Sarey stared at the walls, where outlines of fish had been drawn with names and dates written inside. A wool jacket and raincoat that looked a hundred years old hung from a coat rack made out of deer antlers. Sarey quickly discovered that the steep stairway in the other corner went up to a loft with one small window where she could look out at big pines.

"Can I sleep here?" she called down.

Ma poked her head up the stairs and said, "We thought you might like it. There's a broom downstairs. Let's sweep it out."

So they did a lot of sweeping, carrying out leaves, acorns, and nests made from mattress stuffing. Pa got a face full of smoke the first time he tried starting a fire in the wood stove. He pulled the stovepipe apart and dumped out another squirrel's nest. Then the fire took, and the warmth soon made the cabin feel homey. A June night in northern Maine could be cool.

"Have to get a new section or two of pipe when we get to town again," he said. "The outside pieces are kind of rusty."

Ma had tied her hair back into a braid and was wearing her work clothes: jeans, a tee shirt, and an old pink sweater with holes in the elbows. Usually Ma liked to wear long skirts—not fancy ones, just skirts rather than pants. Sarey sometimes wondered if Ma was pretending she lived a long time ago. But today Ma looked like 1980. She was all business.

"Kitchen first! I wish you could have seen your great-grandmother Potter clean a house, Sarey. No one alive could do it faster or better. She was up on ladders washing windows every spring until she was eighty-five. After that, she would stand there with her hands on her hips, directing me or whoever else did it for her."

Ma took a bucket out to the stream nearby and filled it with water for washing. She wrinkled her nose as she came back into the cabin. "Pretty mousey-smelling in here. I'll need some more cleanser." She opened the bottle of cleanser they had bought when they stopped in town for groceries and poured a generous amount into the bucket. It smelled good to Sarey, like the smell of cleanness. She helped Ma wipe out the cupboards and wash up kitchen stuff. There wasn't much. They had sold so many things before they left the apartment in Buffalo.

Sarey walked over to the sink and turned the rusty faucet. Nothing came out. She looked at Pa, puzzled. His green eyes were twinkling.

"Sorry, Shorty, no running water. Mr. Willette must have left the fixtures there for a joke when he put in the sink. We're roughing it now. Here, come with me." He grabbed a couple of empty milk jugs that were sitting on the drain board and headed out the door. Sarey followed.

Oakley danced beside Pa as he walked up the brook a few yards to a moist, mossy spot where a bright trickle of water joined the larger stream. A little way above, someone had built a pool with rocks. Sarey looked through water so clear she wasn't sure it was really there and watched a little gray salamander swimming over the sandy bottom. She put out her fingers. Instantly, the surface rippled and she felt icy wetness. Pa found a battered blue enameled cup that someone had left there some time before. He rinsed it carefully and offered it to Sarey, full. She thought about drinking in spruces and balsam and emerald-colored moss as the water slid down her throat and made a cold spot in her stomach. At home, water had never tasted like that. Her eyes widened. "It's good, Pa."

"We can take wash water from the brook, but we had best get drinking water from this spring," said Pa. "That can be your job."

Then Sarey asked, "Where's our land, Pa?"

"Let's leave the jugs here on this rock for a minute. I'll show you," he answered.

Pa struck off into the woods going uphill. Sarey followed, breathless and anxious. She thought about wild animals, and her stomach twisted inside her. For a moment she felt as if she were going downhill instead of up.

"Wait up, Pa!" she cried. "What if there's a bear?"

Pa turned and grinned. "It would be more afraid of you than you would be of it."

She had heard Pa say those words before, but they weren't in Maine then. Maine looked wilder than the countryside of western New York. *I bet I would too be more scared than the bear,* thought Sarey. She said nothing, but her stomach muscles clenched as she followed Pa.

Suddenly, she remembered something that she had not thought about during all of the months of planning her escape from Buffalo: she was afraid of the woods. Oh, she loved going

camping with Ma and Pa and Oakley, but when the woods got dark, she heard noises that made her breathing fluttery. At night, she wouldn't go out of the tent without Ma. She was used to street lights, the shine of headlights moving on the living room wall, and the lull of familiar street noises as she fell asleep.

She felt a tiny, niggling doubt. A small voice inside her whispered, *Maybe you're not a country girl.* Heart pounding, she followed Pa.

After a bit, they reached the treeless hilltop that Sarey had seen from the road.

"There was a fire up here years ago. That's why it's called Burnt Hill. The blueberries should be wonderful here." Pa pointed out features on the hillside below them, trying to give her an idea of where their land was.

"Just above that field is the old orchard I told you about. Our woods go to the crest of the hill."

Sarey was confused. All day she had seen nothing but potato

fields and the woods around the cabin. But from here she saw farmland, looking like one of Gramma Harris's quilts, stretching away down the big open valley. She guessed Pa knew which was their land.

"Look over here, Shorty. You can see all the way to Canada."

They walked another hundred yards to where the hill began to fall away on the other side. Before them, in the gathering dusk, under a sky touched with pink, were trees—miles of trees, nothing but trees—all the way to the dim horizon.

"Pines and pines, and the shadows of pines, as far as the eye can see. . . ." said Pa in his reciting voice.

"What's that?" asked Sarey.

"It's from a poem, "The Pines," by Robert Service. One of my favorites."

A brisk wind pushed Sarey's hair away from her face. She couldn't say anything. She had not known that there could be an ocean of trees filling up her entire vision. She had not known that there were so many trees in the whole world. Fear and a funny kind of joy tugged at each other inside her. She felt little and big at the same time: little for being a tiny speck in it all, and big for being a pair of eyes, to see and know about it, on top of this hill.

Later, tucked into the bed Ma made up for her on the mattress in the loft, Sarey wished Oakley would come up with her, even if only for a little while. But he had just put his feet on the first step of the little stairway, wagged his big plume of a tail at her, and then turned to curl up on the floor beside Ma and Pa's bed.

Eight weeks, Pa had said. Up here in potato country, school started in August and then let out for three weeks in the fall for the harvest because the children made up a good part of the picking crews. In the next two months they would build their house, or as much of it as they could before school started for Pa and Sarey. If only . . . if only it was just the woods she had to get used to. If only she didn't have to go to school. . . .

❧ Four ❧

RAP, RAP, RAP.

Sarey stiffened.

The knock came on the door again. *Rap, rap, rap.*

Oakley woofed. Ma and Pa were making a second trip down the muddy logging trail to fetch gear from the truck. After the first trip that morning, they had said Sarey might stay in the cabin with Oakley if she liked. She looked through her little window and saw a high-school-aged boy with brush-cut hair standing on the porch. Where had he come from? Her stomach knotted. She couldn't talk to him. So, she hid, motionless, in the shadow by the window, until he set something down on the porch and started to walk away.

At that moment she heard Pa's voice, "Here we are, Brad. Didn't Sarey let you in? Sarey!"

Then she had to answer Pa. Hot-faced with embarrassment, she went down the stairs.

"Dad sent me over to see if you need any help, Mr. Harris," said Brad.

"Sure do. Want to help me fetch the last load from the truck?

I have a couple of boxes of books I'd rather not leave down there. Wish I had four-wheel drive."

"Mom sent over some wild strawberry jam. It's really good. Us kids picked the berries." As he handed the pint jar to Ma, Brad grinned a grin so quick and gone, it made Sarey think of a lightning flash.

"That's wonderful, Brad. Tell her thank you for me." Ma smiled warmly at him.

"Sarey, you almost lost me some help I could use," said Pa, giving her a look.

"Sorry," she whispered.

"Don't mind her, she's shy as a trout," Pa told Brad as they strode off together. Already Pa looked as if he belonged here in the woods. He was a big man, wiry strong, and it seemed to Sarey that her Pa could make or fix anything. Today, in his flannel shirt and work pants, Pa walked with a bounce in his step. His thick brown hair looked like he had forgotten to brush it, and above his reddish beard there was excitement snapping in his eyes.

Later, Ma and Sarey went to town. They bought a shining section of double-walled stovepipe and a new broom at the hardware store. As they were standing in line at the grocery store, Ma suddenly said, "Sarey, I forgot the laundry detergent. Would you run back and get some? Just try to find one of the cheaper brands."

There was the old familiar lurch in her stomach, but Sarey knew what a detergent bottle looked like, and she could usually read numbers okay, so that shouldn't be too hard. Was looking at numbers really reading? The detergent bottles were all different colors: red, yellow, and orange. She didn't see the blue kind that Ma usually bought. Next to the red bottle was a light blue one. It was only $2.97 . . . or was it $9.27? But that would be way too much. She looked hard at each number, remembering to go from left to right, her lips moving with the effort. Yes, $2.97. That should be all right. But when she handed it to Ma, her mother frowned. "Oh Sarey, that's not detergent—that's fabric softener!"

Sarey felt her cheeks going as hot and red as if they'd been slapped. The cashier must think she was so dumb! She went back for the orange bottle. The woman behind them in line looked annoyed. Ma saw the price and sighed. "Well, at least it's the right thing."

On the ride home from town, Sarey stared out the windows of the truck. The potato fields were green with young plants. Far and wide the fields lay, across valleys and up over hills. It seemed that every place that wasn't too steep or wet was planted to potatoes, except for their land.

Their land was overgrown pasture and woods. The house site needed to be cleared, and to save money they were doing as much as they could themselves. Pa hired Brad Willette to help. Sarey helped drag and pile brush.

"There's nothing a snowshoe hare likes better for a home than a brush pile," said Pa. That helped make the work fun. Sarey would make the best hare hotel in the world right here on their land and look for their tracks in the snow next winter. Slowly, the heaps of sticks grew and sunlight streamed into the clearing. They worked every day until dusk.

"There's no spring on our land. We have to have a well, and that means an electric pump. Besides, I'll need power to run my tools," said Pa, tugging at his beard. "Later we might put in a phone, but we can save money if we don't do that just yet." Soon there was a new electric pole by the road and two more leading to where the house would be. They smelled of creosote and broken earth.

The path to the house site began at the first electric pole and their brand new mailbox on Burnt Hill Road. At first, when she was alone on the path, Sarey would look back over her shoulders and walk quickly. Oakley wasn't much help. He was more interested in chasing chipmunks than in keeping her company. But she liked to fetch the mail. Sometimes there was a letter from Gramma and Grampa Harris. There, on the path all by herself, she would hold it up to the light and try to make out a few words. But even if it was just addressed to her and not to all of them, she would bring it to the cabin and leave it on the table unopened until Ma finally gave in and read it to her.

Everywhere, ferns and little woodland plants were uncurling themselves and growing. Coming up from the mailbox one morning, Sarey stopped and picked a fiddlehead and tried to unroll it, but it would not open. It crumbled and broke. She suddenly realized that it could only grow open. It seemed like magic. She could see why it was named after the spiral carving on the head of a fiddle. In her mind's eye, she traced the curling wood with a finger. Its shape was just the same.

They worked up a small garden near the road with Mr. Willette's rototiller. Ma and Sarey pulled out roots and stones. Pa brought a truckload of cow manure and some lime. They carried wood ash down from the cabin too, and tilled all those things into the black earth where a brushy thicket had grown just a short time before.

"We can't expect too much out of a first-year garden," said Pa, "but we'll throw in some tomatoes, broccoli, and salad greens and see what happens." What happened was that a woodchuck ate all the broccoli plants before Oakley got wise and ate the wood-chuck. Sarey thought it was amazing that the same jaws that shook the woodchuck dead could also take a cookie from her hand as politely as a lady at a tea party. The tomatoes grew, and it was not long before they had fresh lettuce and green onions.

When they planted some late potatoes, Sarey watched Pa placing the seed potatoes at twelve-inch intervals and protested, "They're so far apart, Pa. Won't we get more if we plant them closer?"

Pa shook his head. "That's not the way it works, Shorty. Everything needs room to grow, especially potatoes."

Just then, Oakley started barking furiously. A huge truck with a trailer carrying a backhoe came roaring up the road.

It was time to dig the cellar hole and make a driveway. Sarey bit her lip as she watched the big, yellow machine strip the pretty knoll of its cushiony mosses, leaving deep, muddy ruts. Balsam seedlings lay crushed in its wake. The backhoe belched choking blue smoke. The new driveway was a raw wound on the hillside. The house site looked like the moon. But Pa's eyes gleamed with excitement. "It will heal over, Shorty," he said to her, seeing her troubled look. "These machines can get a whole season of digging done in a day or two."

But it wasn't a day or two. The great, crashing bucket of the backhoe struck ledge, and two days stretched to five and finally six before the grizzled driver jumped down from his machine for the last time, pulled his cap from his head, spat, and said, "Orneriest cellar hole I ever dug, but she's done, Mr. Harris." Sarey felt dark fingers of worry along the back of her neck as she watched Pa write out a check for three times the amount planned. His lips were tight. He wrote quickly, as if he wanted to get it over with.

Then there was the well, which was drilled soon after the cellar was done. Sarey stared as two huge brothers arrived. "First thing we do is to set up shop," said the one named Ray. He hefted a blue plastic cooler out of the back of his truck, set it on the ground, and opened the lid, revealing what looked to Sarey like millions of cans of grape soda on a bed of ice. He offered one to her, and she took it shyly. Then he passed cans around to Ma and Pa and his brother, Wayne.

The Dinkins brothers both wore greasy jeans. Their flannel shirts hung open over grimy tee shirts, and their sleeves were rolled up over tattooed biceps. Ray's tattoo was a palm tree and Wayne's was an anchor. "Two years in the Navy off the coast of 'Nam," Ray explained when he noticed Sarey staring.

"You're the new English teacher, ain't you?" asked Wayne.

Pa nodded.

"I hope you pick books that have movies made of 'em. My boy, Charlie, don't like to read much."

"But sometimes movies leave out the best parts!" said Sarey, without thinking. "Sometimes they're not like the book at all."

Pa gave her a meaningful look.

Sarey bit her lip. Why did she have to go and say that? It sounded as if she *liked* reading.

"Don't we need to get a water witch or somebody like that to come out and tell us where to drill?" Pa asked the men.

"Nah, you just stomp your foot where you want it, and we'll find water," growled Ray.

"That's what we do, find water," said Wayne. "But if you want, I'll witch it for you."

So saying, he tossed his soda can to the ground and snapped

a good-sized forked branch off the shapely little white pine that Ma wanted to save, near what would someday be the back door. Ma opened her mouth and then shut it again.

Wayne assumed a look like he was listening to something sad on the country radio station, and began to pace heavily around the construction site. Sarey had to stuff back a giggle with her hands. Wayne's breath came in wheezes. His yellow hair clung in strings to his forehead, and sweat beaded up on the fold of flesh at the back of his neck. Sarey kept her hands over her mouth and tried not to breathe. Oakley lifted his ears and softly growled. Everybody stared at the stick in Wayne's hands. He covered the house site and solemnly shook his head.

Then he strode up the driveway to the level spot where Pa always parked the truck. Suddenly he struck a pose that reminded Sarey of a picture of a pointer dog that she had seen in one of Pa's hunting magazines. His hands began to shake, and the stick eerily twisted toward the earth.

Ray let out a huge guffaw. "There's your water, Danny boy! Ain't that nice? Easy to get to as a carrot in a sand pile." And before anyone knew it, Ray and Wayne had backed their truck up to the level spot, the rig was pounding up and down, and they had opened another pair of cold grape sodas.

Pa shook his head helplessly and turned back to nailing together the forms for the concrete foundation footers. "You and I and potatoes can't grow without water, Sarey, and neither can our house. We need water to mix cement, but at five dollars a foot, I hope they don't have to go too far down to find it."

Again Sarey felt the fingers of worry. Back in Buffalo Pa had always said, "Someday, when we have enough money, we'll move to the country and build a house." What if they didn't have enough money? What if they couldn't get a house built by winter?

❧ Five ❧

IT WAS AN EYE-POPPING SPECTACLE watching the Dinkins brothers drill that well. *WHAM–WHAM–WHAM–WHAM–WHAM!* The boom shuddered like a sapling in a brisk wind, its cables whipping from side to side. The rotted fenders of the ancient truck flapped, making Sarey think of fish gills, while the bit worked its way down twenty-five, fifty, one hundred feet . . .

Suddenly, the *WHAM–WHAM–WHAM* stopped and the air was filled with the equally jarring sound of yelling. Pa sprinted up the driveway; Sarey and Ma followed.

"What's wrong?"

"That overcooked noodle of a bit's stuck!"

"What should you do?"

"Gotta jar her loose. Might lose the bit, though."

"Then what?"

"Then we're out of business, and you ain't got no well!"

Ray and Wayne put down their grape sodas and set the rig to yank back on the cable. The boom arched as if struck by a hurricane. The truck reared and bucked until its front wheels cleared the ground with every *WHAM*. The Dinkins brothers' faces went crimson. Even the air seemed to shudder. Ray stepped backward, upsetting his soda and spilling purple froth onto the ground.

"Boiling bilge water!" he sputtered.

"Come on, Sarey," said Pa.

"I just hope they know what they're doing," fretted Ma.

"Of course they do," said Pa. "They've probably been drilling wells all their lives."

One hundred-fifty feet. Two hundred-fifty. Two hundred seventy-five. For three days the Dinkins brothers WHAMMed and shouted and drank grape soda. Sarey worried. Pa and Ma looked at each other a lot but didn't say much. It was Sarey who finally asked it one morning at breakfast: "What if they don't find any water?"

"We'll have a very expensive hole in the ground," said Pa, but his laugh didn't sound right.

There were still a few wild strawberries. Sarey found them growing on the bank by the road and picked nearly a pint of the tiny jewel-like fruit. It took a long time, and she wondered how Brad's brothers and sisters had ever picked enough to make jam. Then she wondered how they could give a jar of that precious jam away. The berries made the tips of her fingers pink, and they tasted like fairy food.

"What you got there?" Reluctantly, she showed Wayne Dinkins her precious harvest. "'Bout enough for shortcake. I'll give you a buck for them berries."

Sarey tried to think. What should she do? She did not know how to say no to a grownup. Miserably, she offered up the container of berries and took the crumpled dollar bill.

"I thought you picked some strawberries," said Pa after dinner.

Sarey looked at the floor. "I sold them to Mr. Dinkins for a dollar."

Ma could see that she wished she hadn't. "It's all right to say no. In fact, sometimes it's a darn good thing to say. Next time you want to say no but have trouble saying it, say, 'I'll think about it.' Then you'll have time to get strong about your answer."

The next day, Sarey stopped as she walked by the Dinkins brothers' truck. The door was hanging open on the passenger side, where a sea of soda cans and candy wrappers threatened to spill out. There, forgotten among the trash, were her strawberries. The fragile fruits were already shriveled and moldy. Sarey burned in anger. The dollar was still in her pocket. Angrily, she pulled it out. She wanted to tear it up and throw the pieces into the truck, but she didn't. Instead, she put it beside Pa's place at supper. "It's for the well," she told him.

In the middle of the next afternoon, the pounding noise stopped. The hillside was strangely quiet. The boom was motion-less. Sarey saw the men working around a large pipe set into the ground.

"Look, Sarey," said Pa. He plugged a cord into the tempo-rary electric box, and water began to gush out of a blue plastic pipe coming out of the metal well casing. Wayne leaned over with a grunt and plunged his whole head into it, spraying ice water all over everybody, but nobody minded. They were too happy and excited.

"I ought to buy you a bottle of champagne," said Ma.

"Nah, don't like the stuff," growled Ray. "Grape soda's all we need."

Later that same afternoon, Mr. Willette stopped by. He was the kind of long, lean person who said ridiculous things with a perfectly straight face, so that you couldn't help laughing. His northern Maine accent sounded old-fashioned to Sarey. His hands were rough and work blackened, but his face was oddly smooth and worry-free. Somehow, he reminded Sarey of the potatoes he grew.

He looked at Sarey. "There, now. I was right. I told the Missus you'd sprout whiskers and a ringed tail from sleeping up in that loft."

Then he turned to Pa. "Who did you find to drill the well, Dan?"

"Ray and Wayne Dinkins."

Mr. Willette looked hard at Pa. "I'll be hornswaggled. Don't tell me they've taken up well drilling now? Last year it was auto repair. Before that, I believe, it was scrap metal hauling, and before that, jack logging."

"What is jack logging?"

"Well, they wasn't exactly their logs.... Don't tell me they actually struck water?"

Pa didn't answer. He was slumped against the truck, laughing soundlessly.

That night, when Sarey was supposed to be asleep in her loft, she could tell by the tension in his voice that Pa was not laughing now. He and Ma were talking about money, low and softly—how much this had cost, how much that would cost. It made her think of something Ma had said in the kitchen that night in Buffalo: "Maybe we should wait...."

Sarey tried not to listen. She thought about how cozy the loft was. It wasn't a room of her own, but it was more her own space than the living room in Buffalo. She did feel like a raccoon, curled up and snug. Ma had given her a lesson on how to raise the glass in the kerosene lantern so she could light it with a match and then blow it out after she got up the stairway. Old Joe smelled oily, but Sarey liked the warm yellow light the lantern cast.

Pa had made a little bookcase by the opening for the stairs,

"So you don't slide down on your noodle in the middle of the night." Ma had brought some books for her and said she might read a little to herself before she blew out the lantern, but they both knew she wouldn't.

She did draw sometimes. Once she had looked up to see a mouse with white feet and a long tail, whiskers trembling and eyes catching the lantern light. After a moment, the mouse whisked away down one of its secret passages in the cabin walls. When she looked down, she found him again, bright and quick, in lines that she had drawn almost without thinking. But now the lantern was out and she was supposed to be asleep.

"Do you really think we will be in the house next winter, Dan?" Ma said it softly, as if she was afraid to ask.

There was a long pause while the darkness seemed to think its own thoughts.

"Maybe not. Everything has cost more and taken longer than we planned. I'm going to tell Brad tomorrow that I can't afford to keep him on for the rest of the summer. I hate to do it, but we just cannot pay him. Look how much these windows cost, and I'll be darned if I'll put in cheap ones, the way winters are up here."

"I think it would be fun to stay in the cabin all winter. Think what an experience it would be! We'd never forget it."

"Oh, it would be an experience, all right. But Sarey and I would have the dickens of a time getting down to school when the weather was bad. Oh jeepers! Either way, I've got to start getting in some wood!"

Sarey stared into the shadows. In a few days it would be her birthday. She didn't want anything if it meant they wouldn't have enough money for the house.

"I wish she weren't so miserably shy," she heard Ma say.

"I was kind of shy myself at that age," answered Pa.

"There is something she needs more than presents and a party," said Ma.

✀ Six ✀

JULY EIGHTH WAS SAREY'S BIRTHDAY. Opening her eyes early that morning, she heard whimpering. She tumbled down the stairs to find a scrawny reddish-brown puppy wavering around on unsteady legs. Sarey stared at her parents in disbelief, but they only nodded, grinning. Ma said, "I found her on the side of the road when I went up to town last week. Brad's been keeping her for us, trying to fatten her up so she would look prettier—more like a birthday present. Oakley's so busy hunting that he's not much fun to play with. We thought you needed a friend, Sarey." Ma's eyes suddenly got bright.

It was funny to see Oakley sniff the pup and raise his lip as she tugged on the fur between his toes. Carefully, he withdrew his foot and stalked over to the door. Sarey scooped her up, feeling ribs through the loose skin and puppy fur. Her breath smelled sweet.

"Puppy breath," Pa told her. "Most likely someone dropped her off to get rid of her. It's hard to believe people will do things like that."

"Don't worry. I'll take care of you," whispered Sarey, and the puppy seemed to understand because she began to chew trustingly on Sarey's nose.

"You just wait," said Pa. "In a few days, she'll be fat and wild and woolly. Doesn't take a pup long to settle in."

The rest of the day was full of delight watching the little dog wobble around and begin to play. The way she ate made Sarey laugh. When she was full, and her belly tight and round, she plopped down on her side and, very suddenly, fell sound asleep with her big-jointed legs out stiff and straight.

Ma managed a small but beautiful chocolate cake in the tin box oven that sat atop the wood stove. They had whipped cream instead of ice cream. Oakley got to lick the bowl, and Ma tore open the top of the cream container and gave it to the pup. Clearly, she had never had anything so good. First she licked it clean, pushing it around the cabin floor with her head almost inside the box and globs of cream clinging to her eyebrows and chin. Then she tore the carton to tiny shreds until she was sure that all of that good taste was gone.

There were more presents after dessert. Her New York State grandmother had sent a new pair of blue jeans and a book about a pony. Her Boston grandmother had sent a ruffled dress, a lot of candy, fancy barrettes, and a plastic bank shaped like a white poodle. Sarey wrinkled her nose and laughed.

Ma sighed, saying, "Maybe I can make the dress over for you to wear at Christmas time. I wish Mom could have thought of something a little more practical. There's so much you could use."

Then there was a set of colored pencils with every color in the world, and a cardboard box full of drawing paper, from Ma.

"I stopped at the printer's office, and they let me fill that box with scraps for free!" she told Sarey. "And it's good-quality paper, too."

Last of all, there was a treasure box from Pa. It was made of a red-colored wood, sanded silky smooth, and smelled—ahhh—smelled so woodsy good! Its lid opened on tiny brass hinges. Sarey held it up to her nose and breathed....

"It's red cedar. Mr. Willette gave me a couple of small boards. I've been saving them for something special. Cedar trees are tough and are supposed to live a long, long time. If you keep your woolens in a cedar chest, the moths will never eat holes in them."

The puppy toddled over and curled up next to Oakley's tail. With a sigh and a look that seemed to say, *oh well,* Oak put his nose on his paws.

Then Pa asked Sarey, "What are you going to name your puppy?"

"Well, Oakley's named for a tree. This puppy is reddish colored and smells good. She's tough. And I want her to live a long, long time and get to be an old lady dog. I think Cedar—like a cedar tree, Pa." Sarey reached out to stroke her puppy's silky ears. Cedar took hold of Sarey's cuff with her needle-sharp puppy teeth and tugged with an absurd growl.

Sarey giggled. "I think Cedar is going to eat up our clothes before the moths do!"

❧ Seven ❧

THE NEXT DAY WAS TO BE BRAD'S LAST WORKING FOR PA, but he said, "I have an idea, Mr. Harris." Looking carefully at his shoes, he told Pa about how he had dropped out of high school because he could not pass English. "I know you said you couldn't pay me to work for you this summer, but you're an English teacher—you're going to replace Miss Pinelli, right? If you could school me nights until the middle of August, I'd build this whole house for you...if you show me how. I want to go to the vocational school, but they won't take me until I get my diploma."

Sarey stole a look at Brad. When he came loping over to the cabin on the path through the woods, he reminded her of a long-legged, half-grown deer. All the boys in Buffalo had long hair, but secretly Sarey thought Brad was handsome even with his brush-cut hair. She couldn't believe anyone so smart looking could be dumb like her.

Pa set his level down, picked up the water jug, and took a long drink. "Is that what you want to do, Brad? What about the farm?"

"Joey and Mike can farm it, Mr. H. They like it. Dad says he don't care. Farming is hard. If I want to carpenter, I can carpenter."

"That school ever give people second chances?"

"Oh sure, but Dad says he can't pay for summer school. I can go back to high school and try to pass English next fall. Or maybe I should just go up to Presque Isle and find some other job."

Sarey looked at Brad curiously. There were funny patches of red on his neck, and the small muscles around his mouth were working. He was blinking his eyes.

"You don't know a whole lot of carpentry yet." Pa said it kindly, but Sarey knew it was true. She had seen Pa patiently re-doing angles with the saw and pulling nails with his crowbar where Brad had made mistakes.

"I'm strong. Somebody's got to want me. I ain't going to go back to school next year and be no nineteen-year-old dummy." Brad said this last so fiercely that Cedar whimpered and scrambled over to Sarey's seat on a pile of boards. Sarey tried to imagine herself at Brad's age. Would people call her a dummy?

There was a long silence while Pa watched a red-tailed hawk circling over the treetops and Brad scuffed his work boots in the dirt. Finally, Brad raised his head and spoke carefully, as if he had been working it all out.

"Yeah, I want to go to that school. Ben Whitney went to and he makes real good money now." He paused. "So, will you coach me in English if I stay and work for the summer?"

Pa smiled and nodded. "Sounds like a good deal, Brad."

So they all worked—Ma and Pa, Brad, and Sarey, too. There came to be a cellar built of cinder block and then the framework of sills and joists for the ground floor. Sarey learned a lot of building words, and she even pretty much knew how to spell them (though she wouldn't have said so) because Pa drilled Brad on them, and she listened.

Sarey helped nail down the hemlock floorboards. They were rough-cut and green. Sap spat out as the nails were driven in. "They'll shrink, but green lumber is a lot cheaper. We can lay down a smooth, tight, finished floor over this one later," said Pa.

Blam, blam! "Oh no, Pa!" Sarey's nail was bent over almost to the wood.

Pa pulled it out with the crowbar. "Here, Shorty, hold your hammer further down on the handle and try to swing straight on. And don't nail so close to a knot." After that, more of Sarey's nails went straight. It felt important to be part of building their house. Her nails would always be there, helping to hold it together.

All day Pa and Brad talked about English.

"I stacked them two-by-sixes real good for you, Mr. Harris."

"Yipes!" answered Pa. "*Those* two-by-fours. And, say *well*, Brad; *good* can't modify a verb. It doesn't matter at home, but employers often judge us by the way we speak.

"This hammer feels heavy as lead; I'm sweating like a horse; and I'm as hungry as a bear. What kind of expressions are those?"

"Comparisons using like or as, Mr. Harris."

"Also called?"

"Similes."

"And do you hear those phrases a lot?"

"Yeah."

"So they are almost boring?"

"Yeah."

"So, what else are they?"

"Clichés, Mr. Harris."

"How about this: I'm as hungry as a lumberjack at a tea party."

Brad grinned. "That's a simile, but I guess not a cliché, Mr. H."

"Good."

Sarey listened with a strange feeling that she didn't recognize at first. She didn't like Pa laughing and joking with Brad instead of her. She didn't like it when Pa praised the things Brad wrote at night when they worked together at the table in the cabin.

At noon, they wolfed down sandwiches and drank lemonade, and then Pa brought out his battered copy of *Huckleberry Finn*. "It probably should be Nathaniel Hawthorne, or someone like that, but I think you'll like Twain better. You can learn the difference between dialect and standard English. The more you read, the easier it will get." Then he and Brad took turns reading, Brad uncertainly, and Pa in a tone that made you see pictures in your mind of Huck's freckled face and the raft and the sunlight on the big river, and made you laugh as if it was Huck's own drawling voice telling the story.

Sarey kept her distance sullenly. She didn't dare come too close in case Pa asked her to read, too, but Pa acted as if she was not even there. She lay down on the edge of the canvas tarpaulin that covered the lumber, letting Cedar chew on her fingers, and listened to it all with closed eyes. She pretended that Pa was reading just to her. If only he would keep reading on into the lazy afternoon, with the sun making the stack of two-by-four boards smell so golden and spicy. But, at one o'clock he closed the book and stood up, rubbing his back, ready for work.

Ma was asleep, curled up under her favorite little pine tree. She had trimmed the broken branch smooth and painted the cut with tree tar. White pitch had run down the trunk in sticky drips, but it would be fine, Pa said. Lying there sleeping, Ma looked different to Sarey. She looked almost as if something could hurt her, and Sarey wished Pa wouldn't say, "Back to work, gang!"—so that Ma could go on sleeping a while.

"Did your father ever read to you, Brad?" Ma asked.

"Nah, he don't read much, except farm journals—I mean, he *doesn't* read much, Mrs. Harris. But Ma reads to my sister. That's a really good book Mr. Twain wrote. I think it's the best book in the world."

In the afternoon, Pa asked Brad questions about what they had read, and again Sarey sulked. She knew the answers, too! Why didn't Pa ask *her* any questions?

The days seemed long to Sarey, with the grownups doing nothing but work. When she had finished picking up nails and scraps of wood, and Pa didn't have any other jobs for her, she brought out her paper and pencils and drew. She loved to make patterns out of things: a row of carrots in the ground, three white geese flying, or prints for princess dresses and patches for poor girls' skirts. She made stories. One day she found a section of board on the scrap heap and drew a whole story on it, without words, about a raccoon in a rocket ship flying up to space. She showed it to Ma and told her the story.

"This shows where she goes through the meteor shower and the window gets cracked but she fixes it with bubble gum. Then she lands on Venus, and there's a big tree with candy growing all over it, and she likes it so much that she decides to build a tree house and live there."

Ma shook her head. "It's wonderful, Sarey. Do you know you will be a good reader some day? One of the books that I got at the library is all about a raccoon named Rascal. Why don't you try it? I could help you while I'm cooking dinner."

Sarey turned stiff, like an icicle. She knew Ma was looking at her with sorry eyes as she stalked away. She was mad at Ma for trying so hard. She was mad at Pa, too, and especially mad at the world for having books in it at all. Her eyes smarted with tears. She turned around, almost shouting, "I'm just dumb. Everybody wants me to be smart, but I can't be." Then she ran to the thicket of young hemlock trees where she was building a sort of little house out of leftover wood scraps. She flopped onto the ground and sobbed while Cedar anxiously licked away the salty tears.

Later, at bedtime, Ma read the first two chapters of *Rascal* to her without asking her to try to read again. Cedar cuddled up with them. She was sleek and plump now, full of puppy joy. It was hard to believe she had ever been skin and bones. She seemed to know she had found dog's luck in this world. When Sarey put her supper dish down on the cabin floor, she launched herself into it, wagging so hard that she sometimes knocked over the bowl. Afterward, Sarey had to wipe her long ears with a washcloth.

Cedar's eyes were amber colored. Pa said she looked like a mix of setter and retriever. Sarey loved the little round dome of her head and the pretty, white diamond marking on her chest. She yammered at the truck window when Sarey ran into the post office for Ma. Sarey brought her up to the loft at night. It was cozier shared with a friend. Sarey would fall asleep with her arm around her pup.

Oakley was not entirely sure that he liked having a puppy around, especially one who thought nothing of toddling over to chew on his tail whenever she pleased. When he'd had enough, he would fake a ferocious snarl, but he never touched her with his teeth. Cedar just rolled over on her back and showed him her belly, but no amount of teasing could get him to play.

Sarey did love the stories. Ma let her finger run along under the words, and without meaning to, Sarey's eyes followed. Sometimes Ma got drowsy and her voice trailed off in the middle of a paragraph. She would rouse herself, saying, "I guess all this building is making me tired, kiddo. Mind if we finish this tomorrow?"

One night Ma actually fell asleep. Right when the Black Stallion and Alec had just gone overboard! Sarey looked at Ma. She looked at the book. Then, slowly, she took the book out of Ma's hands. Ma didn't wake up. Sarey studied the words: "then he h-e-a-r-d an e-x-p-l-o-s-i-o-n...f-r-a-n-t-i-c-a-l-l-y..."

Her head began to ache. What did it mean? What was it saying? She bit her lip. She remembered what Pa had said to Brad, "The more you read, the easier it will get." Then she remembered that she wasn't going to read ever again. Angrily, she slammed the book closed and hid her face in Cedar's fur.

❧ Eight ❧

THE NEXT DAY, SOMETHING AWFUL HAPPENED. The something awful was that Sarey looked up, and there, emerging from the woods, was Mr. Willette, and behind him was his daughter, Martha. Her short red hair glowed in the sun. Sarey had known Mr. Willette had a daughter her age, but she had not thought of this strange girl suddenly being there, or of having to actually talk to her. She had thought she would meet Martha when school started.

"Thought I'd see how you was coming along, and I figured that these two girls might want to see each other," Mr. Willette called out to Pa.

How do you know what I want? Sarey thought angrily to herself. Pa took Mr. Willette to look over the construction site, and Sarey was left alone with Martha. She did not want to see her at all. Martha must be a full six inches taller and twenty-five pounds heavier, with bright blue eyes that made Sarey slightly dizzy. Next to her eyes, that hair looked the way orange maple leaves did against the blue of an October sky, but Sarey wasn't going to say so.

With a high-pitched yip, Cedar pounced on one of Martha's

trailing sneaker laces. Martha grinned, showing large, white teeth that hadn't completely decided which direction to grow in yet. Both girls laughed nervously.

"You've grown bigger and a lot prettier!" Martha said to Cedar, as she knelt down and received an enthusiastic face washing. She looked up at Sarey, laughing. "You should have seen her when your Ma brought her over to our house. I gave her a bath because she was so stinky!"

That softened Sarey up a little. *Well, at least she likes dogs. But she probably still thinks I'm little and stupid,* she thought to herself.

"Sarey, why don't you take Martha to see your playhouse?" Ma suggested.

Sarey shot angry arrows back at Ma with her eyes. Reluctantly she said to Martha, "It's over here," and led her to the hidey-hole in the hemlock thicket where she had trimmed out branches to

build her house. It was made out of sticks and odd pieces of boards. The door was just an old piece of rug that she had found behind the cabin. As she crawled in after Martha, Sarey's heart sank. There, sitting in a row, were Tuggy, Monkeyshines, and Little Bear. She had forgotten about them. Now Martha would really think she was a baby. Quickly, she pushed them into a corner, but Martha picked up Tuggy and stroked his worn sides.

"He looks just like our hound dog, Buster!" she said, laughing. "Don't you just love dogs, Sarah? Dad makes us keep Buster chained up outside and only lets him loose to hunt. He says dogs are outside critters. Once, I snuck Buster into the kitchen and gave him some cookies. He liked that." She patted the little stuffed dog. "What's his name?"

"Tuggy."

"How come?"

Sarey shrugged. "I don't know. I got him when I was real little. I just always called him Tuggy. No, you don't, Cedar!" She grabbed Little Bear out of the puppy's mouth before Cedar could carry him out the door. "Here's your sockie." She handed her one of Pa's old socks tied up into knots. Cedar pounced and growled, then shook her toy until her ears flapped.

"You should see all my stuffed animals," said Martha. "Dad says I could buy my own potato farm with them. Every birthday and Christmas, that's what I want. Mom says I'm too old, but I don't care."

"I used to have a lot more," said Sarey slowly. "But I had to sell them at our yard sale before we left Buffalo. Pa said we couldn't take them all in the truck, so I just brought my favorites."

Martha looked around and asked, "Did you make all this yourself? Did your dad let you hammer nails? My dad won't let me use his tools. He says I'll bust my fingers, and it's men's work."

"My Pa lets me. I helped nail down the floor for our new

house." Sarey said it shyly, and looked at Martha sideways to see what she thought.

"Wow," said Martha. Sarey could tell that she thought that was neat, so she went on. "My Ma hammers a lot, and runs the circular saw, too, but she doesn't like chain saws." She was surprised at herself. She hadn't meant to say so much. "Do you want to see our swimming hole?"

Martha nodded, so Sarey led the way to the place where they had made a little pool in the brook by piling rocks across. Cedar followed at, or rather, on her heels all the way, making it hard to walk but kind of funny.

"It's really cold," said Sarey. "It feels good when we're hot. Pa screeches like crazy, but he can stay in longer than anyone." They were starting to take their shoes off to wade when they heard Oakley yipping far off in the woods. When he trailed a hare, his voice was high and happy, and when he greeted them coming home, it was with a big deep *wrow—woof*, but Sarey never heard him make *this* sound before. There was a bad feeling to it, as if something was hurting him.

Sarey called to him, "Oakleee!"

Only the same painful yelp answered her. Sarey looked doubtfully at the tangle of underbrush and tree trunks. She had never just gone off into the woods before. *Maybe there is an animal....Maybe it attacked Oakley....What if we get lost trying to find him?* Her stomach tightened as she stared at Martha.

"Is that your big dog? He sounds hurt or something. Let's go find him." Without hesitating, Martha struck out through the trees. Oakley yipped again, and Sarey found herself following.

Martha glanced back. She must have noticed the expression on Sarey's face because she said, "Break some branches and look back every now and then so you'll be able to see which way we came. We can't get lost if we don't cross the brook. It runs down to the road. We could follow it if we had to." Sarey snapped a lot of small evergreen branches as she went. She looked back and saw that the pale undersides showed clearly against the darker green boughs, leaving a trail behind them. She stumbled after Martha, glancing back every few yards, her heart pounding.

They found Oakley with his left foot held fast in a trap chained to a fallen log. He threw himself toward them joyfully, only to cry out as the metal bit deeper into his foot. His toes were bloody. The steel was biting down to the bone. Sarey forgot everything except helping him.

"What do we do? Should I go get my Pa?"

"I think we can get it off him. My brother Joey used to have traps like that," Martha said. "You'll have to hold him 'cause he knows you. I don't want to get bit."

Sarey grabbed Oak's collar with a hand on each side of his face and got very stern with him. "You be good, Oak. Martha is not going to hurt you. She's a nice person. She likes dogs. She's going to get you loose. Easy boy…easy…easy…." She felt a sense of wonder as her own words echoed in her head: *Martha's not going to hurt you….She's a nice person….*

Martha put a foot firmly on each side of the trap, forcing the spring down and the teeth open. With a start and a growl that broke off in a surprised yip, Oak bounded loose and danced circles around the girls on three legs.

"We did it, Sarah!"

Sarey looked at Martha, feeling tears stinging her eyes. Suddenly the awfulness of having Martha there was gone. There was something she had to say.

"Ma and Pa call me Sarey. That's what I like."

Martha said simply, "Okay, Sarey," and her face lit up with one of her wild smiles. Together they unhooked the trap from the log and dragged it behind them back through the woods. Sarey could see the trail they had made. Besides, Cedar and Oak headed straight back, tails waving like signal flags through the brush.

Pa's eyes flamed when he saw the trap and Oakley's mutilated toes. "I guess we'd better take him to the vet. There go another twenty-five dollars, or so, and we just got done with puppy shots and worming. Only thing worse than a leg-hold trap is a leg-hold trapper who doesn't pick up his gear at the end of the season." He slung the trap onto the pile of rubbish that was headed for the dump. "You girls did a good job getting Oak loose and bringing back the trap, too."

"Would you like to see Martha again?" asked Ma as she steered the rattling Gypsy Wagon around a pothole on the way to the vet's.

"Yes," answered Sarey.

"Good," said Ma. "Tomorrow you can walk over to the Willettes' with me. Pa wants a few laying hens, and Mr. Willette has some he can sell. If we walk, you can learn the way."

❧ Nine ❧

WHEN SAREY GOT OUT OF BED THE NEXT MORNING, Pa was already at work building a little chicken house beside the cabin. "We can move it down to our house later," said Pa, "but for now, I'd rather have them close to us at night. I don't think there are too many critters that will come around where Oak-dog sleeps."

Sarey and Ma walked through the woods to the Willettes' farm. Pa kept the dogs at home. "It's not polite to bring dogs visiting," said Ma. She had ten dollars in her pocket. "Keep your eyes open so you can learn the way."

At first, the woods had looked like nothing but woods to Sarey—trees and trees, all the same. But Ma had been teaching her the names. They had made a notebook together, picking leaves and taping them on the pages. Ma wrote the names. Sarey didn't read the writing, but she liked the shapes of the leaves, and she remembered some of the names Ma told her: the broad, deep-lobed sugar maple, and the pointy red maple, the fronds of sumac and ash, and the round leaves of basswood. She learned the difference between balsam and hemlock. At first, they looked the same, but she soon saw that balsam was longer needled and the white lines on the undersides were more distinct. When in doubt, she would find some dried needles and crush them in her hand. Then she knew balsam, because nothing else in the woods smelled quite so wonderful.

The trail through the woods to the Willettes' farm was easy, really. Sarey glanced back, as Martha had taught her to do, to see how it would look coming home. They walked through the pines into hardwoods and after a while crossed a stone wall that was fringed with ferns. They were fully unfurled now, lacy and delicate. After crossing the wall, Sarey and Ma came out into an overgrown field above the farm. Then it was down around the pond and into the yard, where the scraggly coon hound chained to the barn reared up, voice belling with delight at visitors. Every wagging inch of him was aching for petting.

Sarey greeted him: "Hi, Buster."

"Sarey, you should be careful with strange dogs," warned Ma. But Sarey and Buster were already making friends.

"He was wagging. Martha said he's friendly."

Martha and her mother came to the kitchen door. They had been making raspberry pies, so of course there was tea and a taste of pie before dealing with the chickens.

"Are you making out all right up there in the woods?" asked Mrs. Willette. She was a tall, big-boned woman with work-reddened hands, but she eased the slices of pie onto her best bluebird-patterned plates without spilling a crumb. "I've been thinking of you, Sarey. You try on those sneakers of Martha's. They're quite new, but I can't get her to quit growing so fast."

Then she said to Ma, "Have you got cabbage plants? I don't want to make you carry too much back, but I'm going to have to throw them out if I don't find a home for them. You can leave them in the ground until the first hard frost."

Mrs. Willette's tongue was as busy as her hands. She had a funny way of saying things with a little "no?" at the end that seemed to ask if you agreed with her. She also called things "he" and "she" that weren't hes and shes at all, like when she said, "I am sorry for my house. She is a mess from all the dirt these children track in." A comfortableness about her made both Sarey and Ma feel easy. She seemed not to notice that Sarey didn't talk much. Sarey was so grateful to have it not matter that, without thinking, she found herself saying softly, "I like your pie, Mrs. Willette, and your jam's good, too."

The women talked about sewing. "When you get something cut out, come on over and use my machine."

Ma hesitated, "Oh, I don't want to make a nuisance of myself."

Mrs. Willette laughed. "I'm drier for talk than a bunch of kitchen matches in a jar. Besides, if you would show me how to do that smocking, I could start a bonnet for my sister's baby."

After a bit, they went for the chickens. "Brad caught yours and put them in feed sacks this morning. I believe they're a bit put out—wouldn't expect any eggs for a day or so—but they'll be all right." Sarey and Ma untied the twine on one of the sacks and peered in. A baleful eye, among red feathers, glared back at them.

"She looks wicked mad!" Martha laughed. There were four

hens and a rooster, two in one sack and three in the other, all handsome Rhode Island Reds. Martha walked home with Sarey and Ma, the girls taking turns with the smaller sack, the box of cabbage seedlings, and the sneakers. Before they left, Mrs. Willette put a third of a pie wrapped in foil into Ma's hand, saying, "Dan will like that, no?"

Later, they watched the little flock of chickens exploring their new home. The girls named them Harvey, Lavinia, Myrtle, Hattie, and Little Red Hen. Harvey strutted as if proud of the shimmering rainbows in his neck feathers and sweeping tail. Lavinia, Myrtle, and Hattie all looked alike, and, as it turned out, Sarey could never quite tell them apart. They were glossy brick red and seemed to take pleasure in a good heart-thumping panic. If Sarey so much as sneezed, or whenever Cedar yipped, they squawked and flapped. Then there was a lot of clucking while they smoothed and soothed their ruffled feathers back into place. Little Red Hen was small, disheveled, and picked on, and immediately became Sarey's favorite.

Ma cut out a new shirt for Pa, pinned the pieces, and walked over to stitch the seams on Mrs. Willette's machine. Sarey went with her. The hills between their cabin and the Willettes' farm were becoming familiar.

The potato fields were green and bushy. The vines bloomed strange white flowers with purple and yellow parts. They looked like something that might grow on another planet.

Another day, Sarey and Martha stood between the rows in one of Mr. Willette's fields. The hot breeze made the leaves of the potato vines ripple like a green ocean. In the distance, other potato fields shimmered until it was hard to say where the fields ended and the sky began. All through the summer, in rain, sun, or fog, under the earth, potatoes were quietly growing.

I'm growing, too, thought Sarey. She was spending the

night at Martha's house. She had walked over alone on the path through the woods in the dewy morning, carrying her overnight things in a paper bag. She had begged Ma to let her bring Cedar, but Ma was firm. "A big, foolish puppy is not a welcome guest on a farm, Sarey. We've walked the path together twice now. I know you'll be fine."

Ma was right; she was fine. At first, Sarey looked behind her and caught her breath at every rustle in the undergrowth, but it was easy to see the track made by passing feet. Here were the stone wall and the big maple tree, and she remembered the clump of white birches. For a while, she could hear Cedar yammering about being left, but soon that sound was replaced with the chatter of a red squirrel and the calls of two blue jays. She found herself humming and started to feel that each turn in the path, each tree, and every creature was a friend.

Martha was waiting for her. There were wild adventures in the hayloft, swimming in the pond while Mrs. Willette shelled her peas and kept an eagle eye on them, and, later, Indian fights with Joey and Mike under the lilac bushes. Martha did have a lot of stuffed animals. They seemed to take up half of her room. "Mom gets mad as fire at bedtime when I want to kiss each one good night," she said.

Then Martha said, "Let's read in the hammock."

Sarey shook her head.

"Why not?" asked Martha.

So, Sarey had to tell her about Mrs. Carver and Elm Street School, about what her stomach did when she saw words, and about not reading ever again. Martha looked at her curiously. She started to say something, then changed her mind and said, "That's not so bad, Sarey. My mom's family came down from Canada when she was six, and she said she didn't know a lick of English the first day of school. Cried for a week until she learned to ask 'Where's the bathroom?' Mom says everyone has a burden.

Learning English was her burden. Maybe reading is yours. You'll get better at it, if you try."

Sarey grimaced.

"Well, then, what's wrong with rocking in the hammock while I read, gooney bird?"

Sarey rocked with Martha and gazed at the hollyhocks that wandered carelessly out of Mrs. Willette's slightly wild-looking flower garden. She found a pencil, and on the inside cover of an old coloring book drew a pony wearing a dress and pushing a stroller with a baby pony in it.

"Wow!" exclaimed Martha. "I wish I could draw like that. I drew a horse one time, but Dad said it looked like a cow—and it did, too!" She gave a peal of good-natured laughter at the memory. "Nope, can't draw," and she returned to her story.

Martha loved her books. She read with an intensity that involved her whole body. Her lips moved. She twisted a strand of hair in her fingers. Her bare foot beat time with the action of the story.

"That makes three times I've read *Misty*," she announced, stretching backward out of the hammock to pick up a new book. "I think books are like little TVs, only you make up the pictures in your head. Little TVs that you can carry around in your pocket, and there's no commercials, ever!"

"How did you get so good at reading when Brad is so bad at it?" Sarey asked.

Martha shrugged. "Mom says it just came easy to me, and she had more time to read to me than she had for the boys."

"But my parents read to me all the time."

"Brad's a lot better now. Maybe some people just have to work harder at it."

Sarey looked away from Martha and scuffed her toes in the dirt.

The blueberries were ripe. Martha appeared at the cabin door one morning with a pail and a picnic lunch. Ma went with them to the berry patch at the top of the hill. It was glorious to feel the breeze and sunshine and not have to be any place but outdoors. The berries rolled through their fingers, staining them purple. Ma teased them about eating so many. She could tell because their teeth were blue when they opened their mouths to laugh. She called them bears.

The next day, Mrs. Willette, Joey, and Mike went berry picking with them. Talk came easily while they worked.

"After raising my four and seeing a pack of cousins' and friends' kids grow up, I've learned two things," Sarey heard Mrs. Willette say to Ma. "They're all different—and in the end, they mostly come out all right."

Sarey and Ma brought their berries home and made jam and pies on the wood stove. The smell of the cooking berries was an indescribable deliciousness that filled the whole cabin. Sarey and Martha ran back and forth to each other's houses daily now. Sarey learned that brothers were funny, mean, nice, and teasing by turns, and that they could be teased back.

"We live so far out of town, summers used to be boring 'cause there were no other girls to play with."

"I like your brothers. Joey and Mike are funny, and Brad's handsome."

Martha made a gagging face.

"No, really, Martha. I used to think I just wanted a sister, but now I think a brother would be okay, too."

Once, when her parents went to the hardware store, Sarey was left alone with Brad. Her insides felt like waterlogged soap. She guessed that this must be what it was like to have a crush on a boy. When he stopped to rest, she brought him a can of root beer from the cooler.

"Gee, thanks," he said.

He has nice eyes, thought Sarey. They were paler than Martha's, but they had a way of looking carefully at the world.

"Sometimes, when I'm walking home in the dusk, I see flying squirrels," he told her. "Have you ever seen one?"

Sarey shook her head. She couldn't trust herself to speak.

Brad studied the writing on the can of root beer. "Your dad's the best teacher I ever had," he told her suddenly. "If it wasn't for him, I'd...." He didn't finish.

Sarey said, "I know."

Brad laughed abruptly. "Hey, you talked!" he said.

❧ Ten ❧

"COME OUT AND SEE THESE STARS!"

Brad had just left, flashlight in one hand and books under his other arm. In three days, he would take his English exam.

"He's coming along," said Pa. "A few weeks ago, he couldn't read much more than comic books, let alone a carpentry manual. He'll do fine now."

The air was sweet and the night sky of early August was deep blue velvet, set with gleaming stars between the spires of balsam and spruce. The Milky Way hung like a veil across the top of the sky. In Buffalo, the night sky always seemed to have a pinkish glow and the stars were dim. *I think I'm beginning to like the dark,* Sarey thought with a sudden sense of surprise. She felt a prickling at the back of her neck as she glimpsed for a moment how far is far, how big is big, and how small is small.

"It really does look like milk spilled on the sky," she said.

"Yes, it does," agreed Ma.

"How many stars are there, Pa?"

"Nobody knows, Sarey."

"When you were little, you used to ask us how they stayed up there, and we couldn't answer that one either," Ma said. Sarey could hear a smile in her voice. "I used to tell you that the angels put them there. Do you remember the little song I used to sing to you?" Ma began to sing softly:

> Why do the stars stay up in the sky?
> What keeps them shining in heaven so high?
> Little girl lies awake wondering why...
> What keeps the stars in the sky?

> Do you think that the night is a blue velvet curtain?
> I think it might be, but I'm not really certain.
> Maybe the stars are made from white satin,
> But what keeps them up in the sky?

> Angels sew them with tiny stitches,
> They throw down the old ones for us to make wishes.
> I wish that I could fly up there so high
> And bring back a star from the sky.

"Do you like it up here in the north woods, Sarey?"

"Yes, Pa."

"Do you miss Buffalo?"

"No."

Suddenly a big meteor flared and flashed a trailing arc across the sky. Sarey held her breath and wished the same wish that she always wished. It was about a laughing baby wrapped up in a blanket for Ma, for all of them. "It looked like a girl with long hair," she whispered, almost to herself. Ma was looking at her strangely. Sarey knew that Ma knew the wish. It was a secret between them that they didn't tell Pa.

"Didn't you wish, too?" she asked Ma.

"I guess now is the time to tell," said Ma slowly. She paused as if not knowing how to say what she wanted to say and then said simply, "Next February, we are going to have a baby."

Sarey felt Pa's arms go around them both. He held them tight but didn't say anything.

"Oh, Ma..." was all Sarey could manage.

"I guess it's not the best time—our first winter here—but beggars can't be choosers," Ma said with a laugh.

"It'll be all right," said Pa. "We can be in the new house by then, with the driveway and the truck handy, and a phone put in, and running water....It'll be all right."

Sarey looked up at the stars again and smiled.

A few days later, Brad was accepted into the construction division of the vocational school at Presque Isle. "I was the last one to hand in my exam," he told Pa, "but I guess I knew most of it. I got an eighty-nine." He patted the paperback stuffed in his back pocket. "Guess no one ever saw me carrying a book around just to read 'cause I like to," he said with a grin. Sarey thought he looked handsomer than ever, the way he held his shoulders back and whistled.

One day Pa went to the lumber yard. He was gone a long time, and when he did come back, it was in Mr. Willette's red Ford with Pa's plywood in the back. They unloaded, and he thanked Mr. Willette and sent Brad home with his father.

Pa said nothing. His mouth was tight. He walked around, putting tools under cover one by one. He didn't look at Sarey or Ma. They walked all the way up the trail to the cabin together without speaking.

Finally Pa said, "The truck broke down. There's too much wrong and worn out for it to be worth fixing. We're going to have to get another one. It will use up the rest of our building money, but if we're careful, maybe we can save enough by winter for insulation and roofing. If I work nights and weekends, I'll get us into the new house by February. I promise."

Ma was starting a fire in the stove. She worked fast, snapping sticks hard, and Sarey could tell she was worried.

"We'll be all right, Dan," she said.

"A cabin three-quarters of a mile up a logging road in the middle of winter is no place for a baby."

"Walking will be good for me. Sarey didn't come any too fast when she was born."

"You can't depend on that! We have wanted this baby for too long to take any chances."

Ma tried to smile. "There's no need to wear yourself to the bone. We'll manage."

She paused and then continued uncertainly, as if she were walking on forbidden ground. "You know my parents would help us out if we asked."

Sarey stared at Ma. Even during their worst times in Buffalo, she had never heard her say such a thing.

"Well, we're *not* asking! They made it clear how they felt about the daughter of a famous surgeon marrying a schoolteacher from a less than wealthy family, and they didn't exactly applaud our decision to move to the wilds of Maine. I'll be darned if I'll ask for their help."

"Dan, school starts soon. You'll be working all day, and at night you'll be correcting papers and making lesson plans." Ma sat down. "We'll have money coming in again, but you'll have no time. I just don't see how you can do it."

"I'll do it." Pa's voice sounded rough, like sandpaper. Sarey put out her hands automatically for the dogs' heads, to rub their ears, and they came willingly. She was trying to rub away the fright and trouble—and that sick feeling that the word *school* made under her ribs.

❧ Eleven ❧

MA HAD SAID THAT IN A SMALL SCHOOL Sarey wouldn't feel lost—but Ma was wrong. When Sarey stood outside Greenwood School on Monday morning and looked at the flood of kids sweeping around her—jabbering, giggling, whispering, shrieking, all friends, each sure of where to go and what to do—it did not seem small, and she felt very lost indeed.

There was a cluster of kids by the door getting ready to play something before the bell rang. They had their fists out in a circle. A girl with blonde hair was hitting each fist with her own, chanting:

> *One potato, two potato, three potato, four,*
> *Five potato, six potato, seven potato, more!*

Each fist that was struck on "more" was out. For a minute, Sarey had a horrible feeling that she might throw up. She felt like the fist was hitting her each time, somewhere in the pit of her stomach. The tears wanted to come. She could feel them right behind the hurt in her throat and the burning in her eyes. She blinked a lot to try to spread out the water so it couldn't spill down

71

her cheeks. Stone. I am stone, she said over and over to herself, keeping the picture in her mind, until she felt hard and cold.

There was a Mrs. Somebody with red shoes who was her teacher and who introduced Sarey-made-of-stone to fourteen pairs of staring eyes as "Sarah-Harris-from-New-York-State. We certainly hope you will be happy here, Sarah. Don't we, girls and boys?" The fifteenth pair of eyes belonged to Martha. They were warm and blue. If it had not been for Martha, Sarey would have run home right then and there.

Sarey-made-of-stone decided that here, against the machinery of school, she would keep on being Sarah. Only at home would anyone know her real name.

"First of all, I need to know where to place you in reading groups," said the teacher. "I would like you each to read a paragraph for me, and as you finish, choose somebody else, until everyone has had a turn."

Sarey felt the ground going out from under her. She remembered something Gramma Harris used to say: "Out of the frying pan and into the fire." This must be what she meant. It was not going to be different here. At any moment now, the whole class would know that she was not only small, but dumb, too.

The teacher asked a boy named Peter to begin. Peter was a reasonably good reader. When he finished his paragraph, he chose another boy, Tony, to read. *Good,* thought Sarey, *the boys will choose each other for a while.* Tony read in a flat voice that didn't go up or down but stayed the same tone, only with spaces between his words as if they weren't connected. It was hard to listen to and the kids began to make little restless sounds—scuffing shoes, snuffling noses, and even a few whispers. Sarey stole a look out the window. Instead of rows of roof lines, there were sloping woods behind the school, with paths made by kids' feet leading mysteriously in among the trees at the bottom of the hill.

She glanced around the room. There were so few desks! There had been four classes of third grade in Buffalo, and each class had at least twenty-five kids. Tony finished, and to Sarey's surprise, called out, "Martha."

The big girl with the bright red hair began to read, and the class got very quiet. She read with expression, threading her way gracefully through the many syllables of the long words with such ease, you might have thought she was telling the story instead of reading it from a book.

Sarey relaxed, listening. It was almost as good as Ma or Pa reading. Then Martha stopped and looked at Sarey encouragingly and said, "Sarey."

Sarey fought the panic, as if it were some dangerous snake-like thing, for endless seconds. She felt everyone's attention shift to her. Just like at Elm Street School, they were all fascinated by her misery.

I won't run, she told herself, but as the moment stretched on, it seemed like she might—until the teacher said in a kind voice, "That's all right, Sarah. Everyone feels shy on their first day in a new school. You can read for me by yourself later."

Why did Martha do that to her? Didn't she remember what Sarey had told her about not reading ever again? Sarey looked angrily in Martha's direction, but then saw with a shock that there were tears in Martha's eyes. Martha hadn't realized that she was serious about not reading. She hadn't tried to humiliate her. Sarey gave Martha a quick, tough smile to tell her that she didn't care and that she didn't hold it against her.

But later, alone with the teacher, it was no better. Sarey felt frozen and burning at the same time. Even with the other kids gone out to the playground, she felt afraid. Afraid of trying, afraid of being dumb. Afraid of the part of herself that wished she was back in Buffalo. She wasn't going to read. Finally, Mrs. Burdick put her hand over Sarey's and said, "Never mind, Sarah."

Sarey let herself become the stranger, Sarah, whose only friend was Martha. Sarah, who did not read, who never spoke unless she had to, and then said as little as possible.

"What's Buffalo like?"

"Okay."

"Are your parents really building a house?"

"Yeah."

"What's your puppy's name?"

"Cedar."

She was the shortest in the class at this school, too, even though she was a year older than many of them. The first time they all lined up for kickball, she saw it, and she could only kick the ball a sideways kick that sent it out of bounds.

After the first few days, Sarey began to be able to tell the other kids apart. There were a few she was sure she didn't like: hard-eyed Mick, for one, and Robert, who smelled sour and sweaty and liked to make rude noises and smirk, and Gina, who would not lower her voice until Mrs. Burdick was forced to raise hers. But there were others who looked sort of nice: Jenny, who was pretty and neat and didn't do a lot of shrieking and squealing like so many of the other girls, and Sam, who made the boys quit throwing pebbles at a toad at recess, and of course, steady, kind Martha.

Often, Pa had to stay at school later than Sarey did, and on those days she rode home on the small yellow school bus that covered the Burnt Hill route. Once Martha and her brothers got off at their house, Sarey rode the rest of the way feeling as separate as if she were still in Buffalo. It was funny how you could be in the middle of a bunch of kids and still feel alone. She would scrunch up close to the window and focus on the potato fields rolling by. They didn't look so green now.

During one lonely ride home, she remembered trying to read for Ma back in Buffalo:

"Try to sound it out, Sarey."

"Kah-now."

"What?" Ma came over to the table, dish rag in hand. She peered over Sarey's shoulder and gave a little chuckle. "Oh, sweetie, that's know — like, to know something. Remember? Sometimes the k is silent."

"How can k be silent?" Sarey demanded. "If it's there, it should make a noise."

"Well, English is funny. It has words borrowed from lots of other languages. The rules aren't always the same. Some words you just have to learn as they are."

"Why can't it be the same all the time? Then I could learn it. K-n-o-w doesn't look like anything, the way horse *or* hat *do. How can I know what it means if I don't have a picture in my head?"*

"But you do know what it means. You just used it correctly in that last sentence you said to me. Try to make a picture in your head of what it means to know or understand something, Sarey, like maybe of a little wise man saying, 'Ah ha!' Remember what Mr. Plaisted said? That's one strategy you can use."

"I don't want to have strategies. I want it to be easy, like it is for everyone else. I hate reading!"

"No, you don't, Sarey. Think how much you love to listen when

I read to you. Someday it will be a cinch, and Pa and I will be calling you 'bookworm.'"

Sarey remembered trying to read with Pa:

"Give it a try, Sarey."
"Jemima Puddle-Duck was a sim-plee-ton."
"Sim-pull-ton."
"Why isn't it spelled p-u-l-l then?"
"It's like purple or staple or maple. Ple says 'pull.'"
"It's stupid. It's a stupid story about a stupid duck. Who cares about a stupid duck?"
"You do, Sarey. You used to love this story when you were little."

She remembered her parents talking:

"Don't push her, Dan."
"It's just that she won't try. Every time she comes to a word she doesn't know, or I correct her, there's a thunderstorm. She seems to expect it to be easy. She won't allow anyone to help her."
"I know. Having a brain that sees things differently makes it harder for Sarey, but it's her fear of making a mistake that's really keeping her from learning to read."
"She ought to know better than to care so much about what the other kids think."
"She's made progress, Dan. She has a wonderful speaking vocabulary. I think the reading will come in time."
"When?"

Then, suddenly, Sarey was crying, and she had to wipe her eyes so the other kids on the bus wouldn't see. She knew they whispered about her, but Martha never mentioned reading now, and never acted as if she were dumb. Martha always had the same open smile for Sarey.

❧ Twelve ❧

SAREY LIKED TO WALK DOWN THE TRAIL from the cabin to the road with Pa in the misty early mornings. Often, she got to trotting and galloping. Today she was being a wild spotted pony with a golden mane that she tossed in the wind. Sometimes Pa would run with her.

"Ow! My side hurts."

"Count your strides and breathe with them, in and out, like this: one-two, out-out, one-two, in-in. It helps."

"How did you learn about running, Pa?"

"I ran track in high school. Grampa used to say that I was literally running away from barn chores when I went to practice, but he never missed one of my meets." He looked over at her and grinned.

Together they ran down the trail, leaping small logs and arriving breathless at the truck. The stitch in Sarey's side was gone.

One of the few good things about this school was that Pa was there, too. It was fun to trade smiles with him when she saw him in the hall. Mrs. Burdick had stopped calling on her to read aloud, but it was impossible to do the other work if you didn't read. And, if you wouldn't read, then you couldn't very well write either.

One afternoon when all the other comprehension work-sheets had been handed in, Sarey's was still blank. Suddenly she could feel the teacher beside her, looking at her worksheet. A chill hit the pit of her stomach. Then she saw Mrs. Burdick's hand take away the worksheet and replace it with a piece of drawing paper. The next thing she knew, her teacher had scooched down on her heels, with her face where Sarey couldn't possibly look away. Her smile was friendly and her voice soft.

"Sarey, I know you understand what we are reading. You are going to make great leaps and bounds this year, but for today, I would like you to finish up by drawing me a picture of Almanzo in his father's barn."

How did Mrs. Burdick know that her real name was Sarey and not Sarah? Just before recess, Mrs. Burdick hushed the class. She held up Sarey's drawing.

"Class, do you realize that Sarey was the only one who an-swered the question correctly about whether or not Almanzo han-dled his father's young horses? As you can see from Sarey's picture, he did not go into their stalls, but he did pat their noses."

There was a general murmur as the kids admired her work. Sarey felt an unfamiliar flush of pride, not only because her draw-ing had captured Laura Ingalls Wilder's description of the beauti-ful colts, but also because her teacher had pointed out to the whole class that she, little Sarey Harris, could be smart! Almost by accident, her eyes met Mrs. Burdick's, and she realized suddenly that she had a new friend.

After that, Mrs. Burdick asked her to draw every day: draw-ings to answer questions about the books they read out loud in class, or Maine state history, or things they had talked about in science class, like the life cycle of a butterfly. Mrs. Burdick even let Sarey draw pictures of math problems. One day she brought in a box of beads and showed the class how to figure out multiplication tables using rows of beads strung on wire. It was messy, with beads rolling all over the floor, but it was fun, and when Sarey saw the three rows of seven beads that made twenty-one, it made more sense to her than written numbers and times signs ever had.

Funny things happened—like one time when the gym teacher had them make the shapes of the alphabet with their bodies, using partners to make letters like H and M. There was so much giggling that Sarey couldn't help bending and stretching into the shapes, too. It wasn't really reading, was it? She checked carefully to see which way the other kids made the letters so she didn't get them backward—but lots of people got them backward, and everybody was laughing.

"Let's spell some words now!" said Mrs. Penn. "Let's spell *potato*."

Sarey froze. *That* was reading. But Mrs. Penn asked her to make a T. You could get that letter upside down but not backward, and Sarey was sure the wide part was on the top. She stood straight, with her legs together, arms outstretched. Martha was supposed to be an O. Her face turned almost purple as she grabbed her ankles and tried to make her legs bend backward to make the shape.

"You look like a pretzel," a girl named Marie said. Martha snorted, collapsing in a tangle on the gym floor.

What was this with alphabets? The same week, Mr. King asked the art class to make alphabets using paints, crayons, even clay. He showed them alphabet picture books, pictures of fancy letters painted by monks for religious books in the Middle Ages, different styles of letters, called fonts, that printers used, and even photos of giant letters made for advertising. "You can make any kind of alphabet you want," he told them. Sarey shivered. Art had always been fun. This sounded a whole lot like writing—and reading. Then, suddenly a picture of an S as a little green snake popped into her head and then an O as a turtle.... But she wasn't going to draw it. That was way too much like writing. Slowly, she reached for the clay. M could be a camel....

Mrs. Burdick hung Sarey's best drawings in the hallway outside the classroom. Her clay animal alphabet was placed with some others in the display case outside the art room. Sometimes Sarey would see older kids stopping to look at them. She overheard Martha's brother Mike saying, "Do you believe that kid? She can draw better than Mr. King."

That was the one thing she had. Nobody in her class could draw like she could. The other kids began asking her to draw for them. The girls mostly wanted horses and unicorns. The boys wanted wolves or bears. Robert asked for a race car, but Sarey wouldn't draw that. Sometimes it got to be a nuisance, and she wished they wouldn't bother her. Even so, it gave her something to hold onto, something to be proud of. She even talked a little with Jenny and some of the other girls besides Martha.

One day, Mr. King gave them a take-home assignment. He handed out drawing pencils and two pieces of paper each, rolled up with a rubber band to keep them from getting wrinkled. They were supposed to draw an animal, from life.

Sarey drew Oakley, as he lay by the door in the cabin. She made tiny kissing sounds, just enough to catch Oak's attention, but not enough to make him get up and come. The pencil felt good in her fingers. It made wonderful soft, black lines. Stroke by stroke, Oakley came to life on the paper—the listening ears, wet nose, and watchful eyes....

In school, the kids made her show her drawing. "That's wicked good," said Sam, looking over her shoulder. Sarey couldn't see how something could be wicked and good at the same time, but guessed that was how people from Maine said they really liked something.

Gina announced in her loud voice, "I'll give you five dollars for that picture."

"But I have to bring it to art class today."

"Well, tomorrow, after Mr. King sees it. That's a lot of money, Sarah Harris. You want it?"

Sarey's stomach went hollow. It was a lot of money, and she did want it. She told herself that she could give Pa the money to help build the house. Still, it was the best drawing she had ever done. She took a deep breath. "I'll think about it," she said.

The next day, Gina had the money, but not all of it. She only had three dollars and twenty-four cents.

"It's still a lot of money," she said, eyes hard, daring Sarey to say no.

The inside of Sarey's mouth tasted like rusty water. She eyed the buttons on Gina's blouse. She remembered Wayne Dinkins and the wild strawberries.

"No, Gina, I don't want to sell my drawing," she said. Gina scowled, but did not argue.

Two days later, Mr. King took Sarey aside.

"Each year our school sends a few pieces of artwork to the state fair. I have never sent anything from such a young student before, but I would like to send your dog drawing. I think it could win the junior art prize. The fair isn't until next summer, but I promise you'll get your drawing back."

It could win the junior art prize! And people from all over the state of Maine would see her drawing! What if she had sold it to Gina? Sarey felt something like a little seed of strength inside her chest swell and burst open.

❧ Thirteen ❧

WITH SEPTEMBER, THE POTATO VINES WITHERED AND DIED, as they should do in that month. The great fields turned brown, and now the furrows could be seen again, deep and long, as if the earth had been combed. It was time to dig the potatoes. School was let out so that the older children could help with the harvest. Some kids used the money to buy school clothes. Some saved it for college. There was a lot of talk: boasting about numbers of barrels to be picked and groaning about aching backs to come.

Pa said he was going to pick potatoes to help pay for the army-green International truck that he had bought to replace the Gypsy Wagon. Sarey was sorry to see the old truck go, but Pa said the new one was in good shape, with only 70,000 miles on it. She named it Truck-a-luck-a for the way it sounded as it rattled down the road, and for luck, too, because maybe they needed it.

Sarey knew that Martha and her brothers, and most of the other kids in her class, would be picking potatoes. "I want to pick potatoes, too," she said to Pa. "I know I'm not very big, but I could do it. I could make some money, too."

Pa shook his head. "The work is just too hard for someone

of your size. Your job can be to stay home and take care of your ma." Sarey felt the seed of strength inside her chest shrivel a little when Pa said that. Ma was going to have a baby, but she wasn't sick, or weak, or anything. She looked rosy, happy, and strong. Sarey frowned. Pa just thought she was too small to help.

On Monday morning, Ma put a wedge of corn bread, a tin of sardines, a lump of cheese, and an orange into a paper bag and gave it to Pa, who tucked it into his pack. He was going down to the valley for the first day of the harvest.

"I'll be back at suppertime," he told Sarey, and gave her a hug. Sarey didn't look at him or hug him very hard. Why wouldn't Pa give her a chance to really help? Then he kissed Ma, told the dogs to stay, and walked off down the logging road. The field they were harvesting was three miles away, and he would have to drive there.

Already, to the east, the sky was gold and the sun was beginning to break through the trees. Inside, the cabin lamp still burned and it was shadowy. Oakley whimpered and looked down the trail, but Ma said, "Stay, boy," so he settled down at his lookout point with his nose on his paws. Cedar wasn't sad though, and she pattered over to chew on Oak's tail.

Ma saw the look on Sarey's face and said, "Maybe next year, kiddo, but it's hard work and not always fun."

Suddenly, Sarey had a bad thought. She didn't dare ask Ma, but she wondered, *Will I have to share my room with the baby?* It wasn't that she didn't want the baby. It was just that she wanted a room of her own so much.

They cleared away the breakfast dishes, but Sarey was still quiet and Oak had not moved, so Ma said, "Let's go pick some apples and make a pie for Pa. He'll like that when he comes home."

They put on their sweaters, took baskets, called the dogs, and walked down to the abandoned orchard, where the grass was long and sandy colored now. The trees were heavy with apples. Pa said he would prune the trees next winter, but Sarey liked it wild, the way it was now.

Oakley and Cedar pranced ahead, the big puppy mouthing at the older dog's collar. Suddenly, Oakley bowed low on his front legs and scampered lightly in a circle, waving his tail. He was playing! Cedar launched herself at Oakley only to tumble over her own front legs as he dodged out of the way. "Look, Ma! Oakley's playing with Cedar!" Sarey called. She was right. As if Cedar had crossed some magic threshold, Oakley seemed to have decided that she was old enough to be a friend.

"Soon we'll have to think about getting her spayed, Sarey."

"Spayed?"

"If you have an unspayed female dog, eventually you have puppies."

Sarey stopped on the trail and looked at her mother. "Puppies would be so cute!"

"I know, but she's a mutt. The puppies would be mutts, too, and it can be terribly hard to find homes for them. You don't want someone leaving one of Cedar's puppies on the side of the road, do you? Pa and I think you should get her spayed."

Sarey didn't answer. It was strange to think about Cedar growing up, and it seemed like such a big decision. A moment later, Oakley ranged off into the woods on the trail of chipmunks while Cedar settled down at Sarey's side to chew on sweet-sour apples.

It was still early for apples. The fallen ones were the ripest, Ma said, so they searched for them through the grass. Sarey missed Pa, and it seemed odd to be out of school in September. She wondered whether Martha and the other kids were having fun and whether they missed her—or did they think she was a baby because she wasn't picking with them? The day went slowly. After lunch, Sarey helped fix the pie, then Ma said she wanted to work on a story now that she had some quiet time, so Sarey went

outside. She climbed her favorite pine tree and sat there for a while, but when she came down and asked Ma, it was still only early afternoon.

Resentfully, Sarey filled the kindling box with dead fir twigs, scraps of birch bark that she found on the ground, and small, dry sticks. Pa liked to have a good supply on hand for starting the fire in the mornings and a little extra in case it rained. Sometimes

Sarey hated her jobs and pretended to forget, but Ma and Pa always reminded her. They said she must learn to help. Well, she did want to help, but not just with chores.

Sarey took the drinking water jugs and filled them at the spring. It was a long way lugging them back to the cabin. In June she had imagined bears behind every tree on the path to the spring, but those imaginary bears were gone now. She thought that if she should see a real bear, she would just walk quietly home and come back for her water later. The spring was a special place. It was peaceful, with only the tiny sound of trickling water. She could see the marks of other creatures—deer, raccoons, and such—that came here to drink. It was like a story written in the soft earth, and she thought, *They can write stories without words. Why can't I?*

She brought the kitchen scraps to the chickens, gave them feed, and filled their water pan. Last of all, she looked into each warm nesting box and collected three big, brown eggs. But Sarey knew she wasn't finished. She looked into the darkest corner under the roosting poles, and there, sure enough, was Little Red Hen's egg.

Sarey felt a little better after her chores were done. The cabin was warm and fragrant with baking pie when she came in with the eggs. In another moment, the dogs ran out barking and wagging. Sarey raced out after them down the trail to meet Pa.

And there he came around the bend with his pack full of potatoes and all of him covered with brown, dusty dirt. The dogs danced and jumped around him. He scooped up Sarey and Cedar, one in each arm, saying, "Hi, pups!" Oakley reared up and put his front feet on Pa's chest and woofed.

Ma was smiling in the doorway when they came up. Pa roared out, "Fee-fo-fum-*fie*, I smell the juice of an apple *pie!*" This made Ma laugh and Sarey giggle.

"Well, how did it go?" asked Ma.

"Not bad at all," answered Pa, slowly taking off his pack. He

sat down in the big, worn-out easy chair and began to unlace his
work boots.

"I picked forty-one barrels—not bad for the first day. 'Course
you should have seen some of those high school boys. Makes you
tired just to watch them."

Sarey's eyes widened. "What do they do with all those
'taters? Who ever eats them all up?"

"Well, they load them into great big trucks, or onto the train
that you hear rolling by way down in the valley, and take them
down to the cities, where hardly anybody has a garden and people
buy all their food at the store. Maine potatoes are some of the best
in the world!"

Then Pa said, "Here's a present for each of you."

Out of the pocket of his old jacket he took something
wrapped in colored leaves and handed it to Ma. From the top of
his pack he pulled the biggest potato Sarey had ever seen.

"Here you go, Shorty," he said. "Do you think you can eat
the whole thing?"

It was huge and pale golden, with crumbs of damp earth still
clinging to it. It was as big as one of Pa's boots. Sarey couldn't even
get her hands all the way around it.

"I don't know," she answered seriously. "It looks like a giant's
potato to me."

"These big boys are usually hollow inside and don't keep so
well," said Pa. "That's why you don't see them at the stores. This
one is big enough to stuff like a chicken, isn't it?"

Ma opened the packet and found three beautiful brook trout
on a bed of sphagnum moss. One was nearly thirteen inches long.

"How in the world…?" she asked.

"Left my rod in the truck," answered Pa, "and I couldn't re-
sist dropping in a worm for a few minutes."

"Well," she said, holding up the larger one, "here's another fine trophy! I guess that soup can wait until tomorrow night. These will never taste better than if I fry them up right now."

"Now, don't go running off with that soup," protested Pa. "I'm so hungry I could eat everything in the cabin, and the dogs besides!" He grabbed Cedar by her loose scruff and pretended to bite her.

"No!" screamed Sarey, laughing.

Pa roared and pretended to bite her, too.

"All right, you wolves," said Ma. "We'll have trout *and* soup, and potatoes, too, soon as I can fix them." Then she said, "Why don't you trace that big trout on the wall? It's the biggest I've seen in a long time."

"Jeepers," said Pa. "They come a lot bigger than that."

"Please, can't we, Pa?" teased Sarey. "And we'll draw the potato, too. Ma said they were trophies."

"Well, okay," said Pa, grinning a little behind his beard.

Sarey looked at the walls where Mr. Willette had drawn outlines of all the big fish he and his boys had ever caught. He had said they should record their fish, too, but they had been so busy building the house that they had not had much chance to go fishing. There was only Ma's twenty-three-inch pickerel from the day they went fishing at the marsh. Pa had drawn in the teeth and eyes to make it look fierce.

Pa found a pencil and held first the trout and then the potato while Sarey carefully drew around each one. Then he wrote: "Brook Trout, 12¾"—Dan Harris, 9/5/80" and "Katahdin Potato, 11"—Dan Harris, 9/5/80."

Sarey and Pa stood back, and Sarey thought they looked very fine indeed drawn up like that. Pa chuckled and said, "Well, that's the first trophy vegetable I ever caught!" Then he looked at Sarey and added softly, "It's amazing what can grow underground. School is going better for you this year, isn't it?"

Sarey nodded. "Mrs. Burdick's nice. And Martha's my best friend." As she said this, she was struck with wonder. In all her life, she had never had a best friend before. And even though she wasn't reading, she wasn't failing, because Mrs. Burdick gave her credit for her drawings. Still, she wished that Pa would let her pick potatoes.

Before he gave the trout back to Ma to dip in cornmeal and fry, Pa showed Sarey the white edging on the bottom fins. "See? This is how you can tell it's a brook trout."

Sarey touched the speckles, which looked almost like bright paint. "It's an awful pretty fish."

"I'll tell you a secret," said Pa quietly. "Right now, it's not even half as pretty as when it first came out of the water. A trout is magical that way. Some day you'll catch one yourself and see what they really look like."

After Pa washed up in the brook, yowling like a wild man when the icy water hit his skin, they ate a fine supper of trout, garden vegetable soup, and fried potatoes. Just as Ma was dishing up the pie for dessert, there was a knock on the door.

❧ Fourteen ❧

IT WAS MR. WILLETTE. He was "pleased to set down and eat a bite" with them. He winked at Ma and said he had planned it that way. He looked over to where the dogs had fallen back to sleep by the door, bellies upward, feet in the air—the picture of comfort. He shook his head and chuckled. "Dogs in the house! Ain't that wicked?" He leaned over, rubbed Cedar's belly, and scratched Oakley's ears. Sarey knew he didn't really think their dogs were wicked; it was just his way of saying they were very lucky dogs. But it sure was another funny way to use that word.

Pa had told Sarey that Mr. Willette was kind to let them stay in his cabin rent free, that it was helping them get ahead, and she must always be polite to him. Now Sarey listened while the men talked. They were talking about moose.

"Seen one at dawn yesterday." Mr. Willette leaned forward as he wiped his mouth on the paper towel Ma had given him for a napkin. "The state hasn't allowed moose hunting for a long time, but they've opened a season on them this year—for six days, starting next Monday. I guess they reckon there are enough of them now. Only issued seven hundred permits, and I was lucky enough to get one of them. I aim to have me a freezer full of moose meat, come winter. Lots better than deer meat, any day." He waved a hand in the direction of the clearing. "That moose I saw was heading into your woods, Dan. Tell you what—you see him out there, you don't mind this window, now. You just shoot right through it. Then come get me, and we'll divide the meat. 'Nough there for the winter for both of us. It'd be worth a busted window."

Sarey saw a glint in Pa's eyes. He didn't say yes or no. They got onto the subject of harvester machines then, and how perhaps in the future every farm would have one so they would no longer pick potatoes by hand and gather them in the old split-ash baskets made by the Micmac Indians.

"Seen one of them harvester machines burn up on the Fitzroy farm last season," related Mr. Willette. "'Course, it served them right for working on Sunday. Old Devil got 'em that time!"

After Mr. Willette left, Sarey asked Pa, "Would you really do like Mr. Willette said and shoot a moose through the window if you saw one out there?"

"No." He fluffed her hair gently. "That's no way to hunt, Shorty. But the farmers say moose damage their fields, and the meat can sure help with the grocery bills. Back in the forties, moose were so scarce you couldn't hunt them anymore. They're coming back now. I think a wild thing should only be hunted if the population needs to be thinned, and then only with respect for their wildness. They should be given a fair chance."

Then Pa picked up his book and put his feet on a chair. The next time Sarey looked, his eyes were closed and he was beginning to snore. Ma went over, gently took the book out of his hand and laid it on the table. Just before she and Cedar climbed the stairs up to the loft, Sarey laid her giant potato on the window ledge. Maybe they would eat it sometime, but not quite yet. She wanted to save it for a little while.

&

All the days of that week seemed slow in passing to Sarey. Mornings, Pa's alarm clock would break roughly into the cozy brightness of her dreams while the woods were still black outside her window. She could hear him kind of groan and yawn. Ma would murmur something, and pretty soon he would get out of bed and light the table lamp.

Sarey liked the warm yellow glow that came up the stairs. The dogs knew it meant daytime. Cedar would scramble noisily downstairs, and Sarey would hear Oakley hop lightly down from Pa's chair where he liked to curl up during the night when nobody was looking. Then there was a clamor by the door until Pa let them out.

Sarey would snuggle down in her blankets and listen to the morning sounds: the stove door creaking open, Pa rummaging around for kindling, and the tiny scrape as a match was struck, then the door clanging shut, and—pretty soon—a muffled roaring as the fire took.

Ma would be up by this time; now the cabin sounded really awake. Cupboards and drawers opened and closed. Pans, spoons, and dishes clinked together. It wasn't long before breakfast smells would creep upstairs to draw Sarey out of bed.

Pa was off to work as soon as breakfast was done. Then, even though Sarey was good at thinking up things to play, and Ma had lots to do—sewing for a family growing in all directions, putting away a little garden produce for winter, and working at her writing when she could—always in the back of their minds, they were waiting for Pa to come home.

One morning, Ma pulled out Sarey's winter coat and asked her to try it on. "It's a good thing you don't grow much," she said, looking critically at her. "It can do for a little longer." Sarey didn't think it was such a good thing that she didn't grow much, but said nothing.

Sarey had a house fixed up for her two tiny bears under the

twisting roots of a big hemlock tree that leaned over the brook. The bears had been Ma's when she was Sarey's age. One was brown, one was yellow, and their names were Berry and Honey. Berry was missing an ear. Sarey made them beds in an upper room under a root. At a lower level, there was a kitchen with a flat stone for a table. Using scraps of wood, she had made a dock and a boat for the little bears at the edge of the brook. Hours at a time would go by. Every once in a while, she would stop to listen. Had Oakley barked? Was Pa coming home now?

Evenings were the cozy time. Each day Pa brought a special potato for Sarey. On Tuesday, he brought a tiny, perfect potato no bigger than a blueberry, wrapped up in his handkerchief. It was just the right size to set in an acorn dish for her little bears' supper. She rolled it wonderingly in the palm of her hand and then put it carefully on the ledge beside the giant potato.

"That's how they start out," said Pa. "Just a bump on the root."

The difference in size was wonderful. How could such a tiny thing grow so big from the food and water of the earth? It was something. Sarey looked and looked.

That night, Ma fixed steaming mashed potatoes, baked beans, and cabbage salad. Then Pa read to them about Ratty and Mole while the fire in the stove died down to coals and the dogs slept curled up by the door.

On Friday, Pa had a funny little potato for Sarey. At first, it didn't look like much. He held it out in the palm of his hand.

"See? It's a baby rabbit!"

Sarey was doubtful. It just looked like a potato with a couple of bumps on it to her, but Ma came to the rescue. Reaching into her sewing box, she poked around in it until she found three pins with round black heads. Then, taking the potato from Pa, she carefully stuck them into it, and suddenly there were two bright eyes and a nose. The bumps became the rounded ears of a baby rabbit.

Berry and Honey liked the potato-rabbit, even though she was almost big enough for them to ride on.

Suddenly, Oakley, who had been sleeping under the table, leaped up barking. The fur along his spine bristled and his ears leaned forward. Cedar jumped up, too, listening and looking at Oak, who was by the door now, listening hard and growling.

Pa said, "Must be some critter out there."

They could hear nothing, but Pa lit the lantern and stomped out to check on the chickens. The dogs followed him out, but only Cedar came back with him. They could hear Oakley barking and then growling in the darkness outside the cabin until Pa called him inside.

"Well, whatever it is, it's not bothering the chickens," said Pa.

Ma asked, "Do you suppose it's a bear?"

"It could be, or maybe even a moose, or just a raccoon or a porcupine."

Sarey shivered, but she wasn't really scared, not with Ma, Pa, and the dogs there. It was exciting to think of wild animals out in the night like that. She wished she could hear and smell like Oakley and know what it was.

After a while, Oakley curled up by the door and Cedar sprawled out on her stomach next to him. Soon she groaned comfortably and rolled over on her back, dangling her legs foolishly in the air. They were both asleep. Oakley's paws began to twitch, and he yipped without opening his eyes. He was having a chipmunk-chasing dream.

Pa was watching them, too. After a while, he got up quietly and tiptoed over to the bed. Sarey and Ma stared as he silently drew the dark red wool blanket over his head. Then he got down on all fours and crept toward the sleeping dogs.

He stopped halfway and said, "Grrrr," from way down in his throat. Oakley sprang up with a loud bark, and Cedar began

yapping wildly in her high baby voice. The blanket bear reared up and came closer, growling all the time. Sarey thought Oakley was going to bite, but in another moment, Pa flung off the blanket and both dogs were on top of him, wagging their tails madly and slapping him with their tongues.

Ma and Sarey could not stop laughing; it had been so hard to keep quiet while Pa was playing his trick. It was a good joke, and the dogs didn't mind being fooled at all.

The next day was Saturday, payday for Pa. When he came home, his pack bulged with groceries and he carried a big bag in his arms. There were so many good things: a roasting chicken for Sunday dinner, a pound of butter, a big block of cheese wrapped in white paper, a dozen oranges, a piece of ham, a slab of bacon, milk, raisins, cornmeal, some things in cans, a bottle of root beer, and a bag of popcorn. Last of all were two spools of thread for Ma; for Sarey, a box of watercolor paints with twelve colors and a little brown bag with five sticks of licorice in it; and for the good dogs, two beef bones. Pa's arms were tired!

Saturday was also bath day. While Ma bustled around

putting things away, Pa stoked up the fire, hoisted the washtub onto the back of the stove and filled it halfway. Then he lugged in extra pails of water.

Pa had some news: "Oakley was barking at a moose last night. I found tracks on my way out this morning. They lead up to within a hundred yards of the cabin!"

"Well, that's quite a visitor," said Ma. "No wonder the dogs put up such a fuss."

Sarey had heard tales of moose and seen pictures of them, but she had never seen one. It was hard to believe that something so big and wild and real had come so close in the dark of night. Suddenly, she wanted more than anything to see a moose herself. She made Pa promise to show her the tracks in the morning.

After supper, Ma hung up a curtain by the stove, and first Sarey, then Ma, and finally Pa had a bath. Sarey and Ma soaped up and rinsed in a few minutes. Then they snuggled into their night-gowns and bathrobes and brushed their hair. But Pa took his time.

First, he poured himself a big glass of root beer. Setting the lantern on a chair close by, he then picked up his fishing magazine. Sarey heard the water slosh as he climbed into a tub full of fresh hot water. When at last he wrapped himself in the flannel robe Ma had made him last Christmas, he said he felt like a new man. Ma said she believed he looked like one, too, and they both laughed.

They made popcorn and Ma let Sarey shake the pan. It made a joyous sound, like hundreds of tiny firecrackers. The dogs were at work on their bones, though, and paid no attention to the clatter. Ma got out her guitar and played "The Fox Went Out on a Chilly Night," "Sweet Betsy from Pike," and lots of other songs that Sarey and Pa named. Sarey tried out her new paints, making pictures of the ten little foxes chewing on the bones-o, like in the song, and Sweet Betsy's oxen, big yellow dog, tall Shanghai rooster, and old spotted hog. She didn't know what a Shanghai rooster looked like, but she figured it must be pretty, so she drew its tail feathers with a little stripe of every different color in the box, like a fat rainbow. Pa just sipped his root beer, hummed a little, and gazed up into the shadows, where strings of drying apples hung from the rafters.

The moon was high and big now, almost three-quarters full. It cast a clear light through the window. It seemed to Sarey that the oddly shaped moon, with its pockmarking of craters for eyes, looked just a bit like a potato. Suddenly that reminded her of something. "Pa, did you forget to find me a special potato today?" She tried not to sound disappointed.

Pa laughed and said, "Don't you worry, Shorty. Just go and look in my jacket pocket and you'll find the strangest potato you ever saw! With all those groceries, I forgot about it."

Sarey hopped up and fetched Pa's jacket. There she found a remarkable potato. Sprouting from one main tuber were eleven bumps, lumps, and knobs. It didn't even look like a potato anymore. It looked like a weird animal with many heads and legs and arms of all sizes.

Pa thought it looked something like a walrus, and Ma guessed it was a manatee. But Sarey said no, it had too many heads and limbs. She thought of all the animals, birds, and fish she knew, but it really didn't look like any of them.

"I think it's a *moonimal*," she said.

❧ Fifteen ❧

WHEN SAREY WOKE UP, IT WAS FULL DAYLIGHT. Ma said it was nearly eight-thirty. It was a gray day, with the air damp and still. Pa had gone out walking with the dogs, but Ma said he would be back for breakfast.

She brought out the heavy old bread bowl that had belonged to Pa's grandma. Sarey helped her grate potatoes and squeeze out the potato juice until the gratings were almost dry. Ma measured in baking powder, milk, flour, and eggs. They baked the potato pancakes on a big griddle and kept them warm in a covered pan set over the pot of heating dishwater. Then Ma put more coffee on and fried bacon while Sarey put plates, forks, and mugs on the table.

Pa came back, and he had something for Sarey. It was the tail feather of a ruffed grouse. It was a gentle, mottled brown color, almost like tree bark, with a broad, dark band at its tip. Sarey put it carefully on the window ledge with her potatoes. "It's so pretty," she said. "I wish I had a safe place to keep it."

It was a wonderful breakfast. Ma set out a dish of butter and opened a jar of maple syrup for the pancakes. She even heated

milk, put in just a dash of coffee for flavor, sweetened it with syrup, and gave it to Sarey.

Later, Pa said, "Hey, let's go see those moose tracks!"

They all walked down the trail together. The fallen leaves were soft, muffling their footsteps. The air was sweet with balsam. They had not gone far when Pa stopped and bent down. "There's one."

Sarey and Ma examined the two great half-moons that the moose's hoof had cut into the soft mud. The dogs crowded in and sniffed it carefully. Oakley stiffened and rumbled deep in his throat, ever so softly. Pa laughed.

"Bet Oakley would hightail it for home if he met up with one of those critters!"

Sarey asked, "Are they mean?"

"In a few more weeks I'd say yes. A bull moose in rutting season can be unpredictable, and in the spring, I would stay real clear of a cow with a calf. But I think that most of the time a moose won't bother anybody who doesn't bother it," he replied.

They followed the tracks down to where they came out of the woods. Pa pointed out how long the distance was between strides and how the weight of the big animal splayed the two halves of the hoof far apart and drove them nearly four inches down into the spongy earth.

It wasn't far from there down to the orchard. Sarey gathered up her courage. "Can I go after more pie apples?" she asked.

Pa said, "I really shouldn't leave those birds any longer. I'd best go back and clean them."

Ma said, "I've got a few clothes to wash and hang out to dry before it rains."

Then Pa said, "I don't see why you can't go by yourself, Shorty, if you promise not to bother any moose! Remember, you can always shinny up an apple tree." He gave Sarey a wink.

"Just don't get to daydreaming too long down there," Ma added.

Ma and Pa turned back toward the cabin while Sarey and the dogs continued down to the little wild orchard. The sky was beginning to look heavy, but there was no wind yet and the forest was very quiet.

Sarey shuffled through the grass from tree to tree looking for apples. She picked a few rosy ones from a low-hanging branch. At the edge of the woods she heard Oakley and Cedar. She could tell by Oak's short, high bark that they were chasing something, probably a chipmunk. Then the sound faded and the woods were still again. When she had about a dozen nice apples bundled into a pouch made by pulling up the front of her sweater, she sat down under the biggest tree and looked up into its branches.

Sarey didn't hear the moose, for he made no sound. She just looked up from the wanderings inside her head, and he was there, like another part of her thoughts. He was so close she could smell the vague, warm muskiness of him. Something like fear flashed hotly through her, yet she was not afraid. She sat perfectly still. For a long moment, they stared at each other. At last, the moose's big nostrils began to work the air. He gave one blowing snort, like a startled horse, and turned back into the woods.

That was all. Sarey was left with the clear image of huge, looming antlers; a great, dark, humped body; and eyes that seemed to look at her from a far-off place.

Sarey was thoughtful all the rest of the day. Together she and Ma made a nice big pie, but they couldn't put it into the little oven to bake until the chicken was done. Pa cooked supper. He shooed them out of the kitchen while he worked. It was hard to keep lettuce with no refrigerator, but he sliced a tomato and a cucumber for salad. He made mashed potatoes. It was noisy when Pa cooked. The thumping of the potato masher rattled the windows and woke the dogs.

When at last he pulled out the roasted chicken to make the

gravy, the rich smell made Sarey's stomach rumble. Pa continued to bang around noisily in the kitchen until Sarey and Ma wondered aloud if supper would ever be ready.

"You have to do it right!" he said.

Finally Pa took the pan off the stove and set it on a folded dishcloth on the table. Ma lit a candle because it was Sunday, and Pa said a blessing. It was a good feast. Later, Pa told Sarey to heat water in the skillet with the leftover gravy and scraps and pour it over the dogs' food, so they had a feast, too.

Then Sarey told about the moose. She tried to tell it so that Ma and Pa could make a picture in their minds like the one that would always be in hers. She tried to make them hear the soundless moment, then the snort, and even know the smell of him. A flush rose in her cheeks. She heard her voice flowing clear as brook water in the quiet of the darkened cabin.

"It was like he was a dream creature, but real. He was a shadow and a shape, dark and light all at once. I could see the hairs of his fur. He was like all the forest you can see from the top of Burnt Hill put together and made into one living thing." She stopped, feeling helpless. Maybe words were not enough. Ma and Pa were staring at her.

"That was beautiful, Sarey," Ma said in a hushed voice. "It was as good as one of your best drawings. I wish you would try to write it down."

Pa said, "That was something many people will never see, and very few will see as you did."

Sarey lay awake with the lantern on for a long time that night. She listened to wind in the trees and the steady rain, and she felt the soft presence of the dark. The cabin felt like a safe ship in a stormy sea. She thought about her special potatoes lined up on the window ledge downstairs. They were all different and yet the same. Kind of like people, she thought. She thought about the moose and the other animals in the woods. They lived their secret lives apart from humans, almost in another world. Today she had touched that distant, wild place. The trees outside her window caught the warm light from the lamp downstairs. They seemed like her brothers, reaching up into the night....

Suddenly, she realized that she was not afraid of the woods anymore. It would be silly not to respect the wildness and power of a bear or a moose, but there was a way to understand them without being afraid. You could be safe in the woods if you learned about it and used your brain.

She straightened her shoulders against her pillow, and smiled to think that she missed Martha, the kids at school, and Mrs. Burdick. She almost missed school itself, because maybe, just maybe, at this new school she could be smart. She didn't ever want to go back to Buffalo. Sarey reached for her drawing pad. In steady lines, she sketched the moose and the trees. Then below it, she began to write slowly. "Today I sawe a moose. It was like a dreme creechure, but real. I saw not afrade...."

For a long time she looked at her words. She was not sure whether she had spelled *creature* correctly or not, and she knew she must have made lots of other mistakes, but it didn't make her stomach sick to look at the words. She felt the little seed of strength growing inside her.

✽ Sixteen ✽

THE NEXT MORNING, SAREY CAME DOWN EARLY for breakfast dressed in her oldest jeans and sweater. "I'm going with you," she said to Pa, tilting her chin out. "Maybe we could drop Ma off over at Mrs. Willette's and she could sew."

"Sarey," Pa started to say, but Sarey interrupted him.

"I'm not a baby. How am I ever going to grow up if you keep treating me like one?"

Pa looked at Ma. She raised her eyebrows questioningly back at him. Then Pa grinned and said, "Okay, Shorty. Sounds like a plan!"

When Sarey and Pa got to the potato field, people were already picking. From a distance, they looked like tripod people, bent over from the waist with their legs braced. They were filling big, round baskets. When one was filled, they dumped it into a huge wooden barrel. When the barrel was filled, they put a ticket on it so Mr. Willette could keep track of how many each person filled. Pa got Sarey her own packet of tickets. They were red cardboard, and they all had the number 19 written on them. She was number nineteen.

Sarey saw Martha in tattered overalls and a purple bandana

that clashed with her hair. Her grin was as wide as the potato field, as wide as the blue October sky. "Sarey!" she called.

Sarey thought she'd never done anything as hard as picking potatoes. The first time she filled her basket, she could not lift it. She blinked back tears of embarrassment as Pa helped her dump it in the barrel and told her not to fill it all the way next time. He was working on his fourth barrel before she finished her first.

Joey drove the tractor that pulled the potato digger. The digger had a kind of conveyor belt of long metal rods that rolled under the earth and lifted up the potatoes, moist and pale yellow, and laid them out on the surface. Sometimes there was a tangle of prickly weeds and dead potato vines that had to be sorted through. Sometimes Sarey grabbed for a potato and her fingers plunged right through the skin into a white, liquid, rotten middle. It was the remains of the seed potato. She would hold her breath so as not to smell it, and rub her fingers in the good brown dirt to get them clean again. It seemed funny to wash her hands in dirt, but it worked.

Mr. Willette drove down the rows in a flatbed truck. Mike rode on the back and lifted up the full barrels with a winch. Everything moved slowly and steadily, but with a kind of inward excitement. The harvest was coming in. The more you picked, the more you were paid.

"I see you brought the raccoon," said Mr. Willette to Pa when he saw Sarey, "Don't let her eat too many of them spuds, now!" His eyes twinkled.

"You miss Brad, now that it's harvest time?" asked Pa.

Mr. Willette nodded. "That I do. But I wouldn't change it. He's one happy young man, and he's working hard at the vocational school. It was the right choice for him."

By lunchtime, Sarey's fingernails were broken and filled with dirt. Her legs, back, and arms hurt. But she was picking potatoes and making money. She sat with Martha and the other kids while they ate their lunch. It was kind of like school, but kind of like a party, too, out in the field with nobody to tell them to be quiet.

In the afternoon, the digger broke down. Hurray! Some of the kids even teased Joey while he fussed and banged and swore getting the loose rod back in place. Sarey and Martha laughed and whispered together. Then the welcome rest was over and it was back to the same thing over and over: potatoes, basket; basket, barrel; potatoes, potatoes, potatoes....

That night, in bed, Sarey thought the only parts of her that did not hurt were her nose and ears. When she closed her eyes, she saw potatoes. But she had made fifteen dollars, and tomorrow she would do it again. She was tired, but instead of going right to sleep she carefully adjusted the lantern enough so that it burned a little brighter without smoking. Quietly, she reached over and drew a book from the shelf, *The Cat in the Hat*. The words did not jump as she read them. They lay smooth and flat, one after another. She understood them, and her stomach did not hurt.

✿ Seventeen ✿

PA WAS MAKING LESSON PLANS. Ma was writing at her small makeshift desk in the corner under the stairs. Sarey was drawing. It was raining too hard to pick potatoes. Too much rain could make the harvest drag on until the ground froze, but after a week of work, Sarey was glad to have a day off.

Suddenly, there was a lot of woofing and wagging by the dogs, and in came Mr. Willette for a rainy-afternoon visit. The first thing he did was unload his shotgun, place the two slugs neatly on the table side by side, and prop the gun against the wall close by. He draped his wool jacket over the back of a chair by the stove to dry.

Pa got him a cup of coffee, steaming and black, the way he liked it. The two men sat down at each side of the table in front of the big window.

"'Tain't safe to leave her loaded," said Mr. Willette, indicating his shotgun, "but I can slap them two boys in and fire her off quicker than the pig can get out. Seen that moose, Dan? Tracks as thick on the logging road as at Dick La Marre's dairy yard."

Pa said, truthfully, no, he hadn't. Sarey felt suddenly hot, and moved away from the table with her paper and pencils. She could not look at Mr. Willette.

Pa and Mr. Willette talked potato harvest, then fishing. Mr. Willette pulled a folded-up map out of his pocket and began to show Pa where his secret trout pond was.

"But it's not a secret if you show me, Ed," protested Pa.

"Nah, Secret Pond is there for anyone who can read a map. They just don't know there's brookies as long as my forearm up there," said Mr. Willette. "I can tell a good fisherman. You won't tell the world. Besides, they'd still have to find it, and that ain't all that easy." He traced the windings of the trail with a rough finger. "Follow this brook for about a half-mile. Right here there's a big lightning-struck white pine. You got to turn west there. Miss that, and you're gone to Canada!" He laughed.

Sarey was reaching for the gold pencil to draw her princess's crown when she happened to look up beyond the men and out the window. Out of the dripping spruces behind the clearing, a shape was materializing. She froze. It was the moose. Panic seized her and she felt like the big, red, school fire alarm was going off inside her head.

The creature moved closer, browsing on a shrubby willow that grew by the brook. His massive antlers were silhouetted darkly against the misty trees as he raised and lowered his head like a king.

Sarey's eyes moved involuntarily to the gun. *No, don't look there!* she told herself frantically. *He'll see.* Surely Mr. Willette could hear her hammering heart and choked breathing. At any moment, he would look up, grab his gun, load it, and fire. What to do? What could she do? In her mind she could hear the gun boom, smashing the glass of the window. She could see the moose jerking to the ground....

Not *her* moose! Sarey thought quickly. Somehow, she had to scare the moose away without Mr. Willette ever knowing it was

there. Could she slip out the door and throw rocks at it? She doubted whether she could throw a rock that well. No, she had to make a commotion, a lot of noise that would frighten away the moose, but that would draw Mr. Willette's attention inside the cabin, not outside. He must not look out.

Pa and Mr. Willette talked on. Mr. Willette was leaning back in his chair. They were laughing about something. Even the dogs didn't sense the great animal outside. They were slumbering hard. As Sarey looked at the dogs, she suddenly knew what she had to do. They could help.

Silently, Sarey moved toward the bed. No one paid any attention to her. She stood fingering the blanket for a moment, trying to gather her courage. What if Mr. Willette figured out that she scared away the moose on purpose? He would be so angry he wouldn't let them live in his cabin anymore. What would they do? Maybe she would never have that room with the sunny window and pink curtains. Maybe Ma would never have her study.

At any second, Mr. Willette might glance out the window and she would hear the gun. Nausea swept over her. Don't fall . . . But the little seed of strength inside her chest must have started sprouting roots and branches, because she dragged the heavy blanket over her head. Was she really doing this thing? It definitely was not the same Sarey who had come to potato country in June. She crept toward the snoozing dogs....

In another moment, the cabin erupted in wildness. The dogs scrambled up together, barking a full two-dog alarm at this latest blanket bear. Oakley was light as a deer, but the big clumsy puppy, claws scrabbling, rammed full into the two legs of Mr. Willette's chair that were still in contact with the floor. Over he went, hot coffee, chair, and all! His shotgun crashed to the floor.

Pa jumped up, angry.

"Sarah, what on earth do you think you're doing?" demanded Ma.

Sarey slid the blanket down over her shoulders and hugged it around herself. Her cheeks burned as she looked from one stern adult face to the other, but through the window, she could see with relief that the clearing was empty.

Pa helped Mr. Willette to his feet and sopped coffee off the wet map with a paper towel. He gave Mr. Willette one of his own shirts to put on. He was puzzled. His eyes blazed in a way that almost frightened Sarey. "That was rude," he said to her.

Mr. Willette was clearly annoyed, but he tried to joke about it. "Kid's peskier than she looks, Dan. Make my own play out in the barn on rainy days so's they don't drive me crazy."

Pa started to tell Sarey that maybe that was a good idea and she should put her jacket on and play outside. Then his eyes moved past her to where Oakley stood motionless by the door, ears up, hackles raised. A low rumbling came from deep in his throat.

A smile of understanding suddenly flickered at the corners of

Pa's mouth. Winking at Sarey and fluffing her hair gently, he turned to Ma and asked, "I don't suppose there's any pie left?" Sarey saw him whisper something in Ma's ear, and Ma glanced out the window as he helped her get plates and forks and fresh mugs of coffee. Ma turned and gave Sarey a secret smile.

Mr. Willette was friendly again in a dry shirt, with a huge slice of apple pie in front of him. Ma sat down and pulled Sarey close as she joined the men at the table.

"Can't hardly control that kid sometimes. She's a wild one," said Pa, shaking his head, but his eyes were twinkling.

Sarey sighed and looked out the window. In a minute she would have her pie, but right now she just needed to feel the warmth of her Ma's shoulder and her Pa's smile. Inside, everything was warm and tame, but out there, somewhere in the woods, the moose had stopped running and was browsing. He needed to store up body fat, for after hunting season, the long trial of winter lay ahead.

By the time the harvest was over, Sarey had earned nearly two hundred dollars. She used forty dollars to have Cedar spayed. The sorry-looking thing with the shaved tummy that they brought home from the vet's was back to joyful playing two days later.

Sarey insisted that Pa spend the rest of her money on the house. He used it to buy fluffy pink-and-silver rolls of insulation. It was not enough to do the whole house, but it would help.

What she did not tell anyone was that every night, weary as she was, she had secretly been reading by the light of Old Joe.

✆ Eighteen ✆

I⟳ WAS LATE O⟳CTOBER, and they could look back on a good harvest. "If nothing else, there will be plenty of potatoes to eat," joked Pa. The mornings were frosty, and the ruts in the logging road were skimmed with ice, like panes of glass. Geese flew overhead, and colored leaves covered the trail with a carpet that smelled wonderful when wet and crisped deliciously, like walking in corn flakes, when dry. The wood ferns were faded ghosts, but Sarey found the promise of next spring's fiddleheads in hard nubs at their roots.

There were pictures of their first autumn in Maine that would stay in Sarey's mind forever: a branch of red sumac leaves against a hazy purple hill, mist rising like winter breath off the marsh just south of town, a crow flapping out of a cornfield, feathers spread like black fingers against the sky, and of course, potatoes. Potatoes, cold and damp in her fingers, coming out of the frosted ground, baskets full of potatoes, barrels full of potatoes, and trucks full of potatoes going down the road to the funny looking, half-underground barns that people around here called potato houses.

It was a time of colors and it was a time of feelings.

There was a feeling of excitement, of getting ready. *It was coming any day.* From the window of the school bus, Sarey saw people stacking firewood. Horses, looking woolly, stood with their rumps to the wind that blew down from Canada. At the grocery store one day, she saw a man buying a big jug of something with a picture of a car on the label. She studied the word above the picture: antifreeze. Walking up the logging trail by herself, she heard a last flock of geese, flying southward high and fast. They sounded like a pack of dogs barking. She spotted them finally—tiny black specks, looking like a scattering of pepper on the sky. There was that wistful feeling, too, like when a good friend has to go and you know you won't see her again for a long time. That was the feeling of saying goodbye to summer.

It was Saturday, and they had to work on getting their wood cut for the winter. Sarey looked at Ma and realized suddenly that she was getting fat. There was no doubt about it. She was big in the middle, and she huffed when she bent to pick up logs to stack on

the woodpile. Now and then she stopped to rub her knuckles into the small of her back. But there was brightness in her eyes that Sarey loved to see.

"Good thing there are plenty of standing dead trees," said Pa. With Mr. Willette's chain saw, he felled the trees and cut them into stove lengths. He split the biggest pieces with a sledgehammer and wedges. Sarey and Ma lugged the wood back to the cabin and stacked it in the woodshed. After a while, Pa stopped to get a drink of water. "Well, what do you think, Shorty?" he asked, handing Sarey the jug. "Do you miss your old home?"

Sarey laughed as she said, "No!" Then she added, "There is one thing I do miss. That's how you would take me skating at the rink in the winter. This winter, I wish you would take me skating."

As the weather grew colder and Ma grew bigger, Pa worked harder. After school, he worked on the house until he was late for supper. Evenings, he fell asleep correcting papers.

"I'm afraid you'll have an accident, working late like that," Ma fussed. "That's when they always happen, when you're tired and overworked. And it gets dark so early now."

By late November, there was enough money to buy more plywood, rafters, and roofing. Pa covered what he could with plastic, but often he had to knock away ice and brush off snow before he could work.

On warmer afternoons, Sarey and Ma helped. Pa wouldn't let Ma do anything heavy. Sarey stood in the skeleton of her new bedroom, looked through the rectangular opening of the window, and saw it like a picture of hills and trees, and the great valley spread out before them. She was standing inside the dream room that she had imagined for so long! All it needed was walls and a roof to make it real. It was going to be a nice place to live. Even if she had to share, it was a million times better than the living room couch in Buffalo. Still, she wished that the room could be all her own. But she couldn't think how to say that to Ma and Pa without making them think she didn't want the baby.

There were lots of snowshoe hare tracks around her brush piles. Sarey pretended that the hares were playing cards and having a cozy time deep in the tangle of branches, laughing at Oakley and the rough-legged hawk that sometimes threw a shadow on the snow as it passed overhead.

Pa was tired. "I wish I could spend more time with you, Shorty," he said. There was no bounce in his step now. Often she heard him get up in the night to put wood on the fire. She covered her head with the blankets when she slept, but sometimes her nose got cold. It was hard to climb out of her warm nest to dress in the icy dark. Ma began laying out Sarey's school clothes on a chair downstairs so that she could dress by the wood stove. Frost made winter ferns on the windows, and Sarey tried to copy the beautiful patterns on paper. As long as the fire was going, the cabin was warm, but when the wind blew hard, cold breaths seeped through the cracks and up through the floor.

After a fresh snowfall, Pa and Sarey had a job tramping through it to the truck, but the woods looked like a fairyland all dressed in white. At first, winter looked only black and gray and white to Sarey, but then she began to see colors: pinks and purples in the sleeping tree buds, browns in bark, violets and blues in the shadows on snow, all the changing tones of the sky, and, of course, the many shades of the evergreens.

One night, supper got cold waiting for Pa. Ma couldn't seem to find anything to do with herself. She washed all the dishes in the sink, and still Pa did not come. She gave Sarey her supper and took out a pair of Pa's pants to mend. It grew quite dark, and still there was no Pa. Ma's mouth became drawn in a straight line. She finally said, "Let's go see what's keeping him, Sarey." They put on their things and took the lantern, Old Joe, and started down the logging trail. Shadows swung crazily among the trees from the lantern light, and Sarey could feel Ma's fear. It was like a cold hand on her neck. She knew what Ma was wondering. Ma was thinking maybe Pa's ladder had slid out from under him because of the ice. Maybe he had cut himself horribly with the circular saw. Was he bleeding to death, or unconscious? Something had to have happened. Pa was never this late.

They were almost at the side trail that led to the clearing when they saw a flashlight shining. It was Pa, walking wearily home in the dark. Sarey thought Ma would hug him in relief, but instead her words were sharp.

"You had us scared to death, Dan. If it's going to be like this, maybe we should just try to rent an apartment in town or go back to Buffalo."

Pa said nothing.

❧ Nineteen ❧

CHRISTMAS WAS COMING, and Ma said, "Sarey, don't expect too much this year. Your grandparents won't forget you, but your Pa and I just can't buy much now. We're sorry, but try to think of having our own home soon as a kind of Christmas present."

On the first of December, Miss Baxter, the music teacher, marched Sarey's class into the gym and lined them up on risers. She passed out slips of paper. On each was written two lines of *A Visit from St. Nicholas,* by Clement C. Moore. The kids looked at each other.

"Class," Miss Baxter said in her high, clear voice. "In addition to your carols, I thought it would be fun if you recited this poem, which I think you all know, for the Christmas concert. This is good practice in projection and enunciation, which will help your singing." Sarey's slip of paper began to flutter in her hands. Miss Baxter continued, "There are twenty-eight couplets in the poem and, of course, only sixteen of you. Who would like to recite twice?" She held up the extra slips of paper. A bunch of hands shot into the air. Sarey studied the gym floor while Miss Baxter selected people. Then Martha raised her hand.

"Miss Baxter, Sarey doesn't really like to do this kind of thing. I could say her lines for her." Sarey gave her a grateful look.

Miss Baxter shook her head firmly. "No, Martha. It's very important that you all take part. I am sure Sarey will do very well. Now let's give it a run through. Deep breaths! Andrew, you're first. One, two, three, go!"

"'Twas the night before Christmas, and all through the house...." began Andrew.

Sarey caught Martha's glance and saw sympathy in her blue eyes. Her throat went dry. Jenny leaned over and whispered, "It's okay. You can do it!" But she couldn't. Four lines before her turn, her stomach turned over and she fled to the girls' room.

In a moment, she heard Martha's voice behind her. "She's in here, Mrs. Burdick." She felt an arm go around her. Her teacher was silent a long moment. Then she began to speak.

"Sarey, do you know who E. B. White is?"

Sarey nodded. Pa had read her *Stuart Little*.

"Two years ago, Mr. White received the Pulitzer Prize for his work. That's one of the greatest honors a writer can ever hope to achieve. He has received many prizes, but you know what, Sarey? He won't accept a prize in person if he can possibly help it because he is so shy. They would want him to stand up in front of everybody and say something, and he just cannot do that. It's okay to be like that, Sarey. You are like Mr. White. You have plenty to say to the world—you just don't like to be pushed out in front of everybody to do it." Sarey saw tears in Mrs. Burdick's eyes. "I'll speak to Miss Baxter. I have an idea how you could take part without performing."

So it was that, while the rest of the class practiced their lines, Sarey worked on set design for the concert. Mrs. Burdick and Mr. King helped her put up a paper backdrop. She could choose two helpers to work after school. She chose Martha and Jenny, but Martha broke out laughing and shook her head. "Better not pick me, Sarey Harris. I'm your friend, but I'm no artist!" So, Sarey called Sam instead. Sarey drew the lines and the three of them painted in the shapes together. Sam and Jenny proved to be good workers.

On the night of the concert, Sarey was allowed to stand by herself backstage. Finally, the house lights went down. The curtain opened. In the pause before the kindergarten kids marched on to sing "Jingle Bells," the audience saw a winter scene. It showed a clearing in the woods, just like the clearing where Sarey and her family were building their new house. Behind paper snowflakes suspended on threads were big pines, strong and handsome, lifting armloads of snow, and spruces trimmed in white, like ladies with heavy skirts. In the middle, a balsam fir stood by itself, decorated with corn, berries, and nuts, and all around were the woodland animals: squirrels, foxes, raccoons, deer, snowshoe hares, and, of course, back in the trees, the great, dark, heart-stopping silhouette of a moose—Sarey's moose.

There was a moment of stunned silence and then a general murmur and chorus of *ahh*s. Sarey tucked that sound into the "Forever" drawer in her memory. She could see Ma and Pa and Mr. and Mrs. Willette in the audience, and Mrs. Burdick, Martha, and her class over on the bleachers, faces lit not only by the reflection of the footlights, but with pride for her.

When the program was all over, there were hugs. *I belong here*, Sarey realized. A little part of her went spinning and dancing across the stage. *I belong.*

Sarey wrote secretly to Gramma Harris, and Gramma sent her the old date-nut cookie recipe they all loved so much. Gramma said Grampa was fine and promised they would come visit after the baby was born. Then she added, "Sarey, your writing has gotten so much better! Good for you." There was a five-dollar bill tucked inside the letter because, Grandma said, "Dates and nuts are expensive." Sarey hid the letter.

"What are you making?" asked Ma.

"Date-nut cookies," said Sarey.

"Well, how ever did you know how to do it?" Ma looked at her oddly.

Sarey said nothing.

The next day, Pa cut a balsam fir tree and stood it up in a bucket of water in the corner. "Oh, Pa, look!" cried Sarey. In the upper branches of the tree was a small, neat bird's nest lined with long, brown hairs. Moose hairs? Sarey couldn't believe it.

"I thought you would like that," said Pa with a grin. Sarey did. She got Honey and Berry and put them into the nest. Then they strung popcorn and cranberries and made an aluminum foil star. Ma had brought a few special ornaments. Sarey unwrapped each one, remembering Christmases in Buffalo. There was the tiny cardboard crèche with a picture of Mary, Joseph, and baby Jesus glued inside. The green glitter on the roof was mostly rubbed off now. It had hung on Ma's tree when she was a little girl and was her favorite.

They made blown eggs out of the big brown eggs from the Rhode Island Reds, and Ma produced glitter, glue, and silver and gold paint in tiny bottles to use for decorating them. They made some of the eggs into birds with wings and tails made from blue jay and grouse feathers that Ma had saved. When they were hung on the tree, Ma said, "They are just as pretty as glass ornaments."

On Christmas Eve, they walked through the woods to the Willettes' farm. They feasted on venison and potatoes roasted over apple-wood coals, Mrs. Willette's seven-layer salad, and so many other good things that Sarey couldn't remember them all. Martha's blue eyes shone above her freckles. The two of them hid down behind the Christmas tree and shared wishes: a stuffed monkey for

Martha, art supplies for Sarey, a pony—well, maybe not a pony, Santa couldn't bring that—a sled, skates… Sarey said it so softly that Martha had to say, "What?"

"Skates."

Then Mrs. Willette played carols on the old upright piano, and again Sarey found it surprising to see her large-knuckled, worn hands move so nimbly. She made some mistakes, but nobody cared. Everyone sang, except for Mike, who tried to play his trumpet.

They walked home by lantern light, with the snow glistening around them like a zillion diamonds. Tiny sparkles drifted down from the sky. It was snowing diamond dust! The old coat pinched too much in the armpits to wear anymore—she *had* grown—but Sarey was warm enough in two sweaters. Their boots creaked in the dry snow.

"They say the animals can talk on Christmas Eve," said Ma. Sarey looked calmly into the dark of the winter woods knowing that it wasn't black and dead at all, but full of living things.

Pa walked on ahead, and soon yellow light spilled invitingly through the cabin windows, welcoming them into its warm inside. When they came through the door, Sarey caught her breath. Pa had lit the real candles on the Christmas tree, and it shone like the August stars, so bright that her eyes started to blur.

She hung her stocking on the deer antlers behind the wood stove. Then Pa took her on his lap just as he did when she was little, but it was Sarey who recited, "'Twas the night before Christmas..." all the way through, without any mistakes.

It was not a poor Christmas at all. Not with date-nut cookies, a corduroy-and-flannel coat sewn for her by Ma, and a small, carved, wooden dog from Pa. Sarey sniffed the little dog and laughed. "It's a cedar Cedar!" she said, showing it to her pup. There were all sorts of wonderful and funny things from the Boston grandparents, and a pair of mittens and a knitted hat from the New York State grandparents. Sarey and Martha had spent a whole afternoon at Martha's house sewing balsam pillows for gifts. There was one for Ma and a tiny one for the baby. Ma was pleased, Sarey could tell. Pa liked his pencil holder made out of a soup can decorated with fabric scraps and glitter. "I'll use it on my desk at school," he said as he gave Sarey a hug.

Then Ma gave Pa her special gift for him. It was the last words from the song they loved, beautifully cross-stitched and enclosed by a little wooden frame: "There's a blessing in a winter storm and getting home once more."

There were bones for the dogs, pancake scraps with maple syrup for the chickens, and suet tied up in an onion bag for the chickadees and nuthatches. There was one more package under the tree for both Sarey and Pa: *skates!* They were not brand new, but Ma said that children grow so fast that Santa sometimes fixes up outgrown skates for someone else. In Buffalo, Pa would rent skates for Sarey at the rink. Those had been brown, beat up, and usually dull, but these were freshly sharpened and polished snowy-white, with new laces. Pa's were hockey skates, a little battered but nicely sharpened.

"Thank you," Sarey whispered, smiling into the shadows under the morning Christmas tree. Pa said, "Next sunny day, I'll take you up to Secret Pond and we'll try them out."

Later, they took a Christmas Day walk to the new house, and there they found six brand new windows in cardboard boxes and a front door with a big red ribbon on it. Ma looked startled for a moment. "How did you...?" she started to say. Then she hugged Pa. "They're beautiful!"

❧ Twenty ❧

Two days later it was sunny, and even though it was school vacation, Pa announced that he was not going to work on the house. He was going to take Sarey skating!

"It's only twenty degrees out. Won't you be cold?" Ma asked.

"We'll bundle up. We can start a fire, and the walk through the woods will warm us, too," answered Pa.

"Well, I hate to be a sissy, but I don't relish falling on the ice. I guess we'll stay home and relax," said Ma. She patted her round tummy.

Ma filled a thermos with cocoa for them and made up sandwiches. She put a small blanket with the lunch in Pa's pack. Then she helped Sarey dress in two pairs of socks, the old woolen snow pants they had found at the thrift shop, a sweater, her new coat, then her hat, scarf, mittens, and boots. Sarey felt like she had on a suit of armor to protect her from the cold.

With the dogs bounding around them, they headed up along the brook to Secret Pond. Cedar was big now, on her way to becoming a good-sized dog. Sarey loved to see her barrel through the snow after Oakley, her tongue hanging out and her long ears

flapping until they slapped each other in the air above her head. Oakley could outrun her easily, but stopped long enough to let her almost reach him, looking back with a doggy grin on his face, before rocketing off through the drifts again. Sometimes they shoved their muzzles right into the snow and sneezed on purpose. Cold and snow seemed to make the dogs crazy.

Later, Sarey was to remember everything about that day as clearly as if it were a movie running inside her head. Tiny animal and bird tracks made patterns on the whiteness. A neat line of larger, round tracks showed where a fox had crossed. Chickadees and nuthatches flitted with soft feather sounds at the edge of her vision, making tiny snowfalls in the evergreen branches.

Pa told her about the tracks as they tramped up the brook as far as the lightning-blasted pine. Then he checked his compass and headed west over a small ridge. Sarey's legs and heart pumped, and the hairs inside her nose prickled with ice crystals, but she was used to the walk back and forth from the cabin to the truck. She felt warm and cozy, and sparkling, like Pa's eyes over his frosted beard.

Secret Pond lay in a setting of feathery balsams, but it was open enough to the west wind to be swept fairly clean of snow. The ice was pebbly in spots and had cracks in it that showed it to be nearly eight inches thick. Near the shore they found patches of black ice that had formed too quickly for air bubbles to whiten it. Sarey brushed away snow and looked through to see leaves and mud and waving pondweed. She felt a fascination in looking into that chill underwater world. Out in the middle of the pond, the ice was quite smooth where the wind had polished it.

Pa built a fire, and they sat on the folded blanket to eat their sandwiches and sip some of the cocoa before lacing on their skates. The new skates fit well. They wobbled uncertainly out onto the ice, getting used to the blades on their feet. Sarey almost cried at first because she had forgotten how. She could remember the flying feeling she had felt at the rink in Buffalo, but she did not feel like she was flying now.

Pa said, "Don't worry, Shorty. It will come back to you. You're lucky you learned when you were little. It will always come back to you. It's harder for me. I never tried it until I met your Ma and she insisted on taking me skating. I thought I'd break my neck at first, but I found out it really is fun."

Pa skated with a stiff-leggedness that he could not seem to shake. Soon Sarey found her balance and began hesitant little glides down the ice. The ice made a strange groaning noise, and she looked at Pa in alarm. "What was that?"

"Ice monsters," whispered Pa, but Sarey noticed that his eyes were laughing as he said it, so she demanded a better answer. Pa explained, "Ice contracts and expands with temperature changes. That's what makes these cracks, but there is no danger of us falling through. Look here, you can see how thick it is. You could drive a car out on this. It's just that it's getting a little colder now, and the ice is talking."

Oakley busied himself scouting in the woods, but Cedar watched Sarey and Pa from the shoreline anxiously. Finally, Sarey coaxed her onto the ice and got her to play tug-the-mitten. They began a crazy dance, tugging, laughing, and spinning up and down the small pond.

Pa had to sit on a log and rest his legs. "Skating sure uses different muscles," he moaned. He lay back on the log and Sarey plopped down in the snow beside him. Overhead, the bright sky was beginning to whiten. Everything was so still, so silent—just Oakley's occasional yip off to their left somewhere, a light wisp of wind over the pond's frozen surface, and the *scratch, scratch, scratch* of their skate blades as they went flying again. It wasn't perfect ice, like at the rink. Often a rough spot, an air bubble, or a crack would throw them off balance. They stumbled, fell sometimes, and laughed.

They raced. Sarey shrieked and was caught by a clumsy but powerful Pa, over and over again. Then she lay flat on the ice to catch her breath and cool down. She could feel the chill seeping through her clothes. Above was the soundless infinity of slowly swirling clouds. She was floating. Tiny ice crystals fell out of the white sky and melted on her cheeks. They drank the rest of the cocoa.

"Better go soon," said Pa.

"Oh, please, not yet!"

So, they flew and raced again, and Sarey thought, *This time, Pa won't catch me.* She dodged and Pa tried to turn also. But his skate blade must have caught in one of the cracks, because his leg did not turn with him, and he fell hard.

Sarey looked back. Pa was moving, but it was an awful kind of moving, a helpless kind of moving. He was moving around inside of a pain so terrible, he couldn't get out of it, and his face was twisted into a face that Sarey didn't recognize.

"Pa?"

Sarey skated toward him slowly, afraid of what she would see. Pa's lower leg was bent outward above the skate, where it was not supposed to bend. There was a small spot of blood soaking through his wool pants. Sarey heard her own voice talking reasonably inside her head, as if she were deciding what to do about a broken cup on the floor. *Why is there blood? There's nothing on the ice to get cut on.*

Then she knew what was making the blood. Bone had ripped through flesh. Things began to whirl, and she thought she couldn't do this. She would not be able to help Pa. She would panic and run, go somewhere dark…. She felt like Sarey-made-of-stone again. She tried hard for a few moments to make what had just happened not have happened. It didn't work. Her eyes turned to the great wall of trees surrounding the pond….

"Sarey?"

Suddenly, Sarey found herself on her knees, grasping Pa's hand and saying she didn't know what, just saying anything.

"It's okay, Pa." She felt strangely calm now, almost like she was the parent and he was the child. He seemed to gather himself together.

"I can get up." He rolled onto his side and forced himself upright on the good leg. "Give me your shoulder, Shorty." Leaning heavily on her, he tried to go to shore. Sarey could hear him inhale sharply with each motion. He could not put weight on the broken leg. He stopped. He lowered himself onto his good knee and then back down onto the ice, breathing hard. He could not do it.

Sarey watched as he took his knife from his pocket and sliced open his pant leg and long underwear. Already the leg had swelled greatly and looked purple.

"It's mostly bleeding inside," said Pa. He hacked at his skate laces with the knife. "We have to try to get this off." But they could not. The pain was too much. "At least it's looser now," he gasped.

"I'll go get help, Pa."

Pa gripped her arm hard as if to keep her from going anywhere. He spoke in a very clear voice.

"Sarey, you have to get me off the ice. Bring the blanket over and see if you can drag me on that."

Sarey went for the blanket, but when he tried to crawl onto it, with Sarey pulling on him, he suddenly went white and vomited, then lay back.

"Pa!"

He didn't answer. His eyes were open, but it was like he was going away somewhere inside himself. Sarey had to get him back.

"*Pa!*" she screamed, hearing her voice echo from the surrounding hills. She scraped the vomit away fiercely with the blade of her skate. She didn't know what to do. The fire, small and dying out as it was, was too far away. Although Pa didn't look as big lying down, she could not move him by herself.

After a long time, he seemed to focus his eyes again, and his lips moved. Then he was speaking: "I'm going to need your scarf." While Pa directed her, Sarey wound the scarf twice around the bloody place and tied it, not tight, but not loosely either. She didn't like to look at his face while she did it. "Now cover me with the blanket, Sarey. Go and get your boots on. Break a lot of branches off the balsams by the shore. If you put them under me, I'll be all right while you go to get help."

Cedar was whining anxiously, and Oak had appeared from nowhere. He sniffed Pa carefully and then lay down beside him. Back at the pond's edge, Sarey fought the knots in her skate laces. Any other time she would have given up and made Pa or Ma do it. She hurt her fingers, but she got them undone. She put her boots on and then her mittens again. Her fingers throbbed, but with all her strength, she bent branches until they snapped, hurting her hands again. She kept on until she had a big pile, and then she carried them out to the center of the pond in three loads, slipping and sliding in her boots on the ice as she went. Pa did his best to roll so she could work the branches under him one at a time to keep him up off the cold ice.

"That's good enough, Sarey," he said finally. Oak had gotten up, but lay back down again and put his head on Pa's chest. "Now see if you can raise my leg up and slide my pack under it." Afterward, Sarey didn't know how she did that part.

"We'll have to sell out and go back to Buffalo now. I'm sorry. Your Ma is not going to have the baby with us still living up in the cabin. There is no way I can get the house finished now. It was stupid to buy those windows. It was stupid to think we could build a house with so little money." His face was gray, and he was starting to get that going-away look again.

She wanted to scream at him to stop him from talking, from saying those things, but instead she said, "Pa, it's okay. We'll be all right."

"Push Oak closer to me and cover both of us. He will help keep me warm." She tucked the blanket around Pa as best she could, but it was too small.

"Sarey, listen carefully. If you follow our tracks in the snow, you can't get lost. Keep Cedar with you. If somehow you do get lost, walk away from where the sun is setting, and you should come to the brook. Then follow the brook downstream to the cabin. For gosh sakes, don't cross the brook, though—it's wilderness out there! But if you follow our tracks, you can't get lost. Don't try to go too fast. I'll be okay."

"Yes, Pa."

Sarey looked at Pa and he grinned a funny, twisted grin. "I'm okay," he repeated. "Go and tell your Ma. She'll know what to do."

❧ Twenty-one ❧

SAREY WENT SLIPPING BACK ACROSS THE POND to the trail with Cedar close at her heels. Oakley raised his head to watch her go but made no move to follow. She didn't look back again, but plunged into the woods, following the trail they had made coming.

She listened to her breath as Pa had taught her when they ran down the trail together, *One-two, in-in, one-two, out-out. Don't go too fast. Sell out and go back to Buffalo. Don't think. In-in, out-out, in-in, out-out.* In her mind, she saw a picture of rows and rows of gray houses under a gray sky. They would have to leave Maine and go back to Buffalo, back to Elm Street School.... Her world was coming apart! *Don't think!* Her boots made a chuffing sound as they went into the dry snow. Cedar followed at her heels.

Suddenly, the snow was blank before her. She ran faster, stumbling, trying to find the trail. No trail! "Oh God, Pa!" Then his voice was in her head: *Follow the tracks in the snow. You can't get lost.*

She turned and followed her own tracks back. The snow gave way under her feet and she saw rocks and moving water. She looked to either side and saw that, without realizing it, she had crossed right over the little brook on a snowdrift. Then she noticed where their tracks had turned as she and Pa walked out to the pond. She also could see where she had missed that turn a minute ago and plunged straight ahead. She looked up to see the big broken pine, long splintered fingers of heartwood reaching up toward the sky. *Miss that, and you're gone to Canada. This way. This way home.*

The narrow trail of footprints seemed like a plowed road in the vast forest. It was definitely snowing now—tiny, driving flakes. She ran doggedly, feet heavy, tears streaming freely down her cheeks. Down along the brook. Past the spring. There was the henhouse, the woodshed, and the cabin. She struggled with the doorknob, sobbing. It turned in her hands, and there was Ma, startled, looking questioningly over Sarey's shoulder when she saw she was alone.

"Pa broke his leg, Ma! It's bloody. It's bad, Ma."

Then Ma was holding her hard, putting a hand on her hot, wet cheek, feeling her through her clothes almost as if to see whether Sarey was broken somewhere, too.

"Okay. Okay, Sarey." Ma's face went very stiff, and she began to talk as if to somebody who wasn't there. She was putting on her coat that wouldn't button over her belly anymore, and her boots. "It'll be dark in another hour. He'll be cold. I can get to the Willettes' in twenty-five, maybe twenty minutes...."

Then she seemed to see Sarey again. "Did you put the blanket over him?"

"Yes, but it's too small."

"You'd better stay here. I don't know what else you can do."

But Sarey was dragging the big red blanket from Ma and Pa's bed. "He's cold, Ma. I'll go and wait with him."

"Sarey, I don't want you to go back in those woods. It's starting to snow. What if you get lost?"

Sarey felt something inside her go very straight and strong. It

didn't matter that she was only ten years old. She had to do this. She looked at her mother and knew that all of what was inside her was in her eyes.

"If I go fast, I can follow the tracks. I know the way now. He's going to freeze if I don't go."

Ma closed her mouth tightly and took the blanket from Sarey. For a moment, Sarey thought it was all over, and because she was a child and too small to help, Pa would be dead. But Ma turned and folded the blanket in thirds, rolled it as tightly as she could, and tied it with a piece of clothesline. She tied another piece of line to Cedar's collar and then to Sarey's waist. She put a handful of kitchen matches in a plastic bag and put it in Sarey's pocket. Then she shook Old Joe, to see that there was kerosene in his belly, and handed the lantern to Sarey.

Sarey picked up the blanket by the rope. She stood a moment, thinking hard. She couldn't stand it if Pa started talking that way again. Somehow, she had to keep him from talking about giving up, keep him from going away inside himself again. Her eyes strayed to the table, and she noticed the book that Pa had been reading to her the night before. It was *Charlotte's Web*. She put the blanket down for a moment, stuffed the book in her coat pocket, and picked up the blanket once more.

"I'm ready, Ma."

They went out together, Sarey stumbling a little against the tugging of the big pup. Ma grabbed her by the shoulders. "Be careful, Sarey."

Then they went different ways, Ma taking the trail to the Willettes' farm and Sarey back on the trail to Secret Pond.

It was different going back, a long trudge uphill. Sarey was glad to let Cedar tow her along. Did dogs never get tired? Ma would get Mr. Willette, or somebody. It would take how long? A long time anyway. *Don't think.*

She did not cry now, just stubbornly put one boot in front of the other. Back to Pa. There, finally, was the pine and the trail turn. She saw where she had gone wildly off the trail in her panic and almost laughed at herself. It was like she had been someone else then. Someone a lot smaller.

Then she saw something else that made her heart almost stop: fresh moose tracks crossing where she had passed not twenty minutes before. Later she wondered if it really happened that she turned her head to see the huge, dark form behind the veil of falling snow. She thought he paused to look back at her before plunging on into whiteness.

The snow was coming steadily now, and the woods looked ghostly. It was covering the tracks some, and the afternoon was dying quickly. Chilling and dying. But she could still see the trail, and the way looked familiar. Cedar was pulling her along, straining at her collar as if she knew exactly where she was going.

Sarey came out on the shore of the pond and stopped. Where was Pa? Then she saw that he, Oakley, and the blanket were a mound of white on the snowy pond, and she felt afraid.

"Pa?"

She walked toward him. He didn't move. Oakley lifted his muzzle, and his tail, sticking out from under the blanket, thumped twice.

"Pa?"

Then he pushed the edge of the blanket away from his face. He looked tired, almost a forever kind of tired.

"Ellen, I'm sorry. We can try it again in a few years, when the kids are bigger, when we have more money saved."

Ellen was Ma. Sarey shook her Pa's shoulder gently.

"Pa, it's me—Sarey. Ma is getting help. I brought something to cover you better." She brushed snow off him as best she could. When she unrolled the big old wool blanket and spread it out, it covered all of him.

He knew it was Sarey now. "You get under too, Shorty. We have a while to wait yet."

Ever so gently, Sarey crept under the blanket next to Pa. Cedar lay down in the snow and licked her face. It felt so good to rest. All her muscles quivered. Pa took her hand, and suddenly tears began to roll down his cheeks. He was crying now—she had never seen him cry before. She didn't know what to do.

"I'm sorry, Sarey. You and your Ma can't carry all the wood. You can't be fetching water, hauling in groceries. The baby will come soon. We can't stay in the cabin. We can't stay in Maine. There is no money to rent a place. I spent all we had left on the windows. The school can't give sick pay for longer than three weeks. I wouldn't lose the job, but there would be no money. We'll have to go back to Buffalo."

She had to make him stop talking or she would scream, so she said, "Hush, Pa. I'm going to read to you." He stared at her as she opened the book. Cedar was plump and warm next to her. Sarey read:

> The next day was Saturday. Fern stood at the kitchen sink drying the breakfast dishes as her mother washed them. Mrs. Arable worked silently. She hoped Fern would go out and play with the other children, instead of heading for Zuckerman's barn to sit and watch the animals...

The snow began to swirl and fall more thickly. Sarey's body cooled down now that she was still, and then the chill began to creep in, but there was warmth from Pa, and she knew that she was giving warmth back to him. On the other side of him, his good old dog was giving more warmth to him. She stopped when she got to a hard word and spelled it to Pa; he told her what the word was. As it got darker, she couldn't see well enough anymore, so she pulled out the matches and lit the lantern. Old Joe shone brightly in the snow.

> "Perhaps if people talked less, animals would talk more. People are i–n–c–e–s–s–a–n–t..."

"Incessant. Never stopping."

> "...incessant talkers—I can give you my word on that."
> "Well, I feel better about Fern," said Mrs. Arable....

The words began to flow less haltingly. Sarey stopped at the long ones and found Pa's eyes on her. She made him listen to the letters and say it. He had to think a long time before he answered her. She could feel him starting to shiver. After reading for a while, the black words marching across the pages seemed like a trail, like the tracks through the snow to the cabin. If she could just stay on it, if only she could keep Pa following along with her, it would surely take them home. It wasn't so hard. Together, they could do it.

She didn't know for how long she read, but the woods grew black with full night, and the snowflakes hissed on the glass globe of the lantern. Finally, there was a shout and a light on the shore, and they were there—Mr. Willette and Brad, pulling a toboggan, and the two younger boys, and Ma.

❧ Twenty-two ❧

THEY FLEW PA IN A HELICOPTER TO BOSTON that night. The doctor at
the Caribou hospital had said, "We can handle almost any kind of
break here, but the dislocation is very serious. And with a com-
pound fracture, especially in one that has been exposed to the air
this long, there is a major threat of infection. We would like to
send him to an orthopedic surgeon in Portland—unless, of course,
there is someone else you would prefer."

Ma had answered wearily, "My father is an orthopedic surgeon at Massachusetts General Hospital. If my husband has to fly
somewhere, he might as well go to Boston. If Dad doesn't want to
treat him, one of his colleagues can. My daughter and I can stay
down there with my mother."

Ma and Sarey were coming in the truck with the dogs. They
had slept the night in the big double bed in Mrs. Willette's guest
room. Sarey had curled safely against Ma, feeling the tiny kicks
and stretches of the baby under the tight roundness of Ma's belly.
Now suddenly, this new little person growing inside Ma seemed
real to her. She dreamed once that she was reading to Pa. A blanket covered his face, and they were in a helicopter flying forever in
the dark...

She woke up shaking, but Ma murmured something comforting, and she remembered that Pa was okay. The bed was so warm and soft, and she was so very tired... She slept without dreaming then, until Ma woke her to go.

The dogs rode up front, Oakley on the floor and Cedar on the seat between them. Sarey slept most of the way curled up with her head on Cedar, and Ma played the radio softly as she drove down the bleak winter highway. *The radio works in Truck-a-Luck-a, but we didn't have very good luck,* thought Sarey to herself.

They stayed at Grandmother and Grandfather Potter's big house for three weeks. There were many trips on the train to visit Pa in the hospital. The first time, Sarey was almost shy about seeing him. Grandmother had given her some money, so they stopped at a flower shop, where Sarey picked out a pot of tiny yellow daffodils to bring to Pa. They rode up to his floor in an elevator. It took a few minutes to find him. The echoing hospital corridors seemed to go on forever in a maze. *At least in the woods the trees are all different,* she thought to herself.

At last, they peeked around a door, and it really was Pa there in a bed, come all the way to Boston. They had not lost him on the way. The doctors had operated on his leg, which was wrapped in bandages instead of a plaster cast because of the wound. Several times a day, the nurses changed the ice under it and checked for swelling.

Sarey couldn't speak. Pa still looked bad, but at least he looked warm, cared for, and safe.

"Come here, Shorty," he said, reaching for her. "I hurt, but not so much you can't hug me."

Before she knew what she was doing, what she was saying— but not meaning to be rude—Sarey said, "Please don't call me Shorty now, Pa. It makes me feel little. I may be small, but I'm not little anymore."

Pa held her hard for a long time. Then he said, "Would you

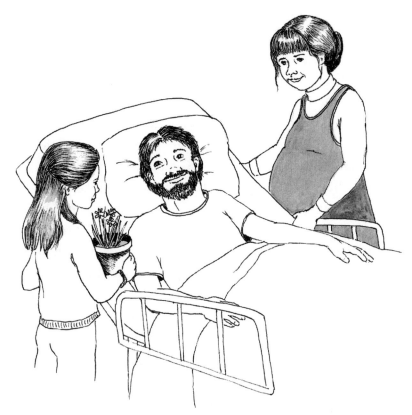

mind very much if I called you Scout? I like to have my own private name for you, and I'd like to always remember how you found your way back for help and brought me that blanket and stayed with me out on the cold ice."

Sarey nodded, then pulled out the card she had made.

Pa read it aloud, "Sticks and stones can break your bones, but words can never hurt you."

Sarey grinned happily at him.

"There's one more thing," said Pa. "When did you get to be such a good reader?"

Sarey could feel her cheeks getting pink. "I was going to show you one day."

"Well, you sure showed me."

Grandmother Potter was happy to have Ma and Sarey at her

house. She took them shopping, to the art museum, and out to lunch at the country club—and all that was fun. Above her artistically made-up face and penciled brows, Grandmother's hair was tinted a delicate bluish silver. She wore a different smart-looking suit every day. Her high heels clicked when she walked. When they went to the country club, Ma and Sarey got dressed up, too, but Ma always seemed to have a strand of hair loose, and she made rolling eyes at Sarey over her menu while Grandmother was talking to the waitress about exactly how she liked her steak cooked.

Sometimes Sarey would read for Grandmother at bedtime. She was only a little bit nervous. She still didn't like to have anyone help with the hard words, saying, "I can figure it out. Just give me a minute." But if she really got stuck, she would look at Grandmother and let her say the word.

Grandmother was amazed. "This child reads very well, Ellen. I don't know why you ever thought she had a problem!" Then she said something that made Ma's eyes get teary: "You and Dan must have been doing something right."

The hard part was the dogs. They were miserable chained up in the backyard. Ma and Sarey took them for walks when they could, but Oakley's tail hung like a flag at half-mast. The fat, sleek, gray squirrels, which lived off sunflower seeds from the neighborhood bird feeders, were the only things that interested him. He watched them, all of his half-wild heart fixed in his brown eyes. Because of the chain, he could never chase one. Sometimes Sarey would sit and talk to the dogs. "You miss the woods, don't you, boy?" she would say to Oakley. She stroked their heads and rubbed their ears the way they liked.

Grandfather Potter was very tall. He looked more comfortable in his blue hospital clothes than he did in a suit or the corduroys and brand-new–looking flannel shirts he wore at home. One day he gave Sarey a tour of the orthopedic wing of the hospital and took her into a little dark room to look at the x-rays of Pa's leg. He explained the surgeries: setting the bones, wash-out procedures, moving muscle from the back of the calf to the place near the shin where muscle had been damaged, to give the bones a better blood supply for healing, and then the skin graft. Sarey was interested in the sharp white shapes that were the pin, screws, and plate holding the bones together, but she was more interested in the fluid shapes of the bones themselves, the way they fitted smoothly at the joints.

"This is what we call a spiral fracture. It's a difficult one to set, especially having broken through the skin. Your father is very lucky. Part of the circulation to his foot was cut off. If you hadn't gotten help for him so quickly, he might well have lost his leg."

Sarey couldn't think what to say. She studied the x-ray film and imagined drawing the ghostly white shapes. "Don't you think bones are beautiful, Grandfather?"

"I certainly do, Sarey. The muscle structure covering them is beautiful, too. The human body is a wonderful thing. Would you like to be a doctor when you grow up? I work with many excellent doctors who are women."

"Sure, or an artist, or a teacher, like Pa. He's the best teacher in the world. Brad—he's the boy who helped us this summer— Brad told me Pa changed his life. He didn't want to farm like his dad, but he couldn't pass English to get into vocational school, and Pa helped him do that."

Grandfather Potter rubbed his lip. "You could get a Ph.D. and be a teacher at a famous university like Harvard, right here in Cambridge—and really be someone."

Sarey looked at her grandfather. "Is it more important to teach grownups than it is to teach kids?"

Grandfather Potter glanced back at her. Then he looked away. "No, Sarey, it isn't. It's just that..." He stopped himself. "No, you are absolutely right. It isn't."

Sarey suddenly put her arms around her grandfather's waist. She felt his hand on her hair.

They were moving back to Buffalo as soon as Pa got out of the hospital. First, though, they would return to Maine one more time—back to potato country and the cabin, and the little half-built house on the side of the hill. Mr. Willette would help Ma pack out their stuff from the cabin. They would put the house and land up for sale.

"I'm a country girl, Pa. I'm much stronger now. I can carry the wood and water."

"I just won't do it, Sarey. There are too many things that can happen with a baby. When you're older, we'll try it again."

"What about Oakley? He'll hate going back to the city."

"He's just a dog, Sarey."

But she heard the catch in his voice as he said it, and she knew that Oakley wasn't just a dog to Pa.

Everybody seemed to be pulling different ways.

"Stay with us. Have the baby here where the best doctors are available," urged Grandmother Potter.

"Having a baby is normal. It's not a medical crisis," Ma answered. "Besides, there are perfectly good doctors in Buffalo."

"But your father and I would love to have you stay here. This is a hard time for you, and we would like to be of help."

"Dan would feel better if we stayed with his parents, Mom. You can understand that. We can put Sarey back in her old school. When Dan gets back on his feet, he can substitute teach until he finds a job, and then we can get another apartment. Who knows, maybe I'll start selling some stories." Ma laughed a little laugh, but Sarey knew it wasn't a very hopeful one.

All Sarey wanted to do was to go home to potato country.

✧ Twenty-three ✧

AFTER PA HAD BEEN HOME A FEW DAYS at Grandmother and Grandfather Potter's house, they said a million thank-yous and headed north. Pa was grouchy. He said his leg felt like it would explode. He was supposed to keep it elevated, and there wasn't much room in the truck to stretch it out or raise it. It was a long, miserable drive. When they got to the Willettes' house, it was almost dark. Brad was there.

"Why aren't you at school?" grumbled Pa.

Brad grinned. "I had a long weekend, Mr. Harris."

The Willettes gave them a late supper, and it seemed to Sarey that something was odd. Why weren't the Willettes acting more sorry that they had to sell out and go back to Buffalo? There were whispers, glances, and tiny smiles. There was something enormous and bright in Martha's eyes, but Sarey was too tired to wonder anymore. She slept in Martha's room; Ma was in the guest room; and Pa slept on the couch with his leg propped on pillows.

"Guess the first thing we should do is go into town to see the real estate agent," Pa said at breakfast.

Mr. Willette had gotten up and gone out early. Mrs. Willette and Brad looked at each other. "I know for a fact that Bill Lester doesn't go into that office till afternoon on Saturdays," said Mrs. Willette. "Why don't we go over to the house with you and help you start packing up your tools?"

Pa shrugged and looked at Ma. "Might as well. I'll be no help, but I'll go along anyway."

So they piled into the truck. Sarey, Martha, and Brad all rode in the back with the dogs. Mrs. Willette rode up front with Ma and Pa. They got to the house and found that the driveway was plowed. Mr. Willette's truck was parked there already. Sarey climbed out of the camper after the others and walked around to the front of the trucks. Then she just stood and stared.

Instead of an unfinished skeleton of two-by-sixes, there in the clearing on the side of the hill stood a little house. It was *their* house, with the walls closed in, the roof on, and the Christmas windows and door in place where there had been only rectangular openings before. There was a big woodpile outside, and smoke was coming out of a shiny stovepipe with a jaunty new cap.

Pa climbed heavily out of the truck, hanging onto the door while he got his crutches under him. His face was expressionless. Ma just stood there, looking. Mr. Willette stuck his head around the door and called, "Why don't you all come in where it's warm?" They went in, and it *was* warm. Brad was dancing around showing things and talking faster than Sarey had ever heard him talk before.

"Here's the light switch. The electrical wiring class did that. The water works—see? You can put a better sink in sometime. This is an old one that was kicking around up at school. You can flush the toilet—it works, too—and there's a place to hook up a washer in the cellar."

Sarey clattered down the stairway to look. It was a room now, where once they had struggled with roots and mud and

S.V.W.B.

ledge, and then with cement and cinderblock. Sure enough, there were shiny faucets and water pipes, reminding Sarey of the sweating, shouting Dinkins brothers and the deep well that had cost so much. She saw, standing side by side in the corner, two bushel crates of big potatoes. Somehow, that made it seem like home.

She dashed back upstairs, peeked into the bedrooms, and then she stopped. There, in Ma and Pa's room, stood the old wooden crib from the Willettes' attic. Every Willette baby, as well as a number of cousins, had slept in it. She turned to look back at the others.

"I thought the baby would have to sleep in my room. I thought I had to share it."

Mrs. Willette smiled at Sarey. "You don't suppose you always slept on the couch in Buffalo, do you? Babies have a way of needing their mothers in the middle of the night. Your Ma told me that you have waited too long for your own room. When the baby is old enough for his or her own room, you folks can add on."

Sarey softly pushed open the door to her own room and stepped inside. Martha followed and stood in the doorway behind her. The winter sun was shining through pink curtains at the window. They had brought down the mattress and bookcase from the loft in the cabin. Someone had found her drawing pad, opened it to the sketch of the mouse, and propped it up next to her books. It was bare now, but it was *her own room!*

"It's wicked pretty," she whispered.

Ma, who had come to stand behind her, laughed and said, "Sarey Harris, you sound as if you were born in Maine."

Brad was still talking. "We only got wallboard up in the bedrooms, but all the insulation is in. It stays warm as toast. Dad is letting you borrow the stove from the cabin until you get your own."

"Brad, how in the heck did you do it?" Pa was smiling now.

"I got a couple of teachers and a bunch of guys from school interested, and they came out on weekends. Mom cooked up some whopper spaghetti dinners. Dad and the brats got the wood in. They even skidded the chicken house down with the chickens right in it. You should have heard the squawking! Did you see it out back? Mom and Martha made those curtains in the bedrooms. Martha said you liked blue and Sarey liked pink, Mrs. Harris."

"Ed, I can't believe this!"

"Ain't much potato farmin' to do in January," drawled Mr. Willette, embarrassed.

Martha grabbed Sarey and squeezed her. "You don't have to go back to Buffalo, Sarey Harris!"

They had brought down the table, chairs, and big bed from the cabin, also on loan. Ma sat down heavily in a chair. "You are very good friends to us. You've done too much. I don't know what to say."

"Ain't nothin' to say. You done a lot for my boy, and that's all there is to it. Around here, one hand washes the other," said Mr. Willette.

There was a demanding scratch at the door. Brad leaped to open it, and in tumbled Cedar, with Oakley prancing behind. Their noses were working and their tails were high as they explored the new space.

Mr. Willette shook his head, but he was grinning. "Lettin' dogs in the house. Looks like they own the place. Now, ain't that wicked?"

Pa found a chair, too, and put his throbbing leg up on the wood box. He looked at Sarey questioningly. "I guess I'll leave it up to you, Scout. It still might be smarter to go back to Buffalo for a while. We have a baby coming in less than a month. Your Ma's going to need a lot of help and I'll be lucky if I can drive her to the hospital when the time comes. There will be firewood to carry, not to mention groceries, laundry, cooking, and cleaning, and not a cent to spare. What do you think?"

Sarey looked steadily back at him. She thought of the woods and the moose. She thought of the potatoes when they came tumbling out of the ground, firm and golden, ready to last the winter in a snug cellar. She was strong now, unafraid of the wild world, the people world, or the world of written words. The little seed of strength inside her had grown into a sturdy, living thing that would always be there.

She thought of the baby growing inside Ma, ready to come out soon, too. Ma and Pa, the baby, and the dogs—her family— they belonged here. She thought of their good neighbors, the Willettes, people who believed in helping each other. And she thought of her special friend, Martha, and her teacher, Mrs. Burdick.

Sarey's eyes found a cardboard box next to the door, full of things from the cabin. Sticking out from the top were the lantern, Old Joe, and the little cross-stitched piece in its frame that Ma had made for Pa at Christmas. Silently, Sarey picked up the lantern and placed it on the table. They all watched as she found a hammer and carefully drove a small nail into the wall above the place where a couch would go, when they could afford one. Still without speaking, Sarey hung the cross-stitch in place. Then, in a firm voice, she read the words aloud: "There's a blessing in a winter storm and getting home once more."

She looked at her parents, smiled, and said, "I think we should stay."

The End

❧

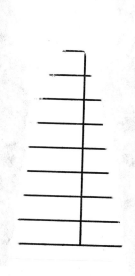